GORILLA
MONSOON

JOHN LONG

CHOCKSTONE PRESS
EVERGREEN, COLORADO

1989

Published by
Chockstone Press, Inc.
Post Office Box 3505
Evergreen, Colorado 80439

LIBRARY OF CONGRESS CATALOGING-IN-PUBLICATION DATA
Long, John, 1954-
    Gorilla monsoon / John Long.
        p.   cm.
    ISBN 0-934641-03-X
    1. Adventure stories, American.   I. Title.
PS3562.049434G6   1989
813'.54--dc19

Foreword

IT WAS DENVER, a meeting of the board of directors of the American Alpine Club. John Long was a board member, though he had never yet made it to a meeting. Nor would he be coming today. "He's in Brazil filming *King Kong*," the Alpine Club president said.

"Is he *playing* King Kong?" a wag asked. Everyone laughed.

In the last letter I got, John Long – or as he's affectionately known, Largo – said, as to why he'd asked me to write the foreword to his book, "Lastly, you don't know me personally, and this is important. You see, it's the damndest thing, but people tend to focus more on me than on my work, and in so doing the work gets relegated to a secondary issue, while the 'Largo' image grows absurdly out of proportion."

What John doesn't remember is that we did meet once, on a climbing weekend in Joshua Tree, California, at a campfire. Of course I knew all about John Long, and of course I was overwhelmed by his presence and size. But I was also chagrined. Because, due to his vast musculature, I found myself surprised that every time he opened his mouth, complete and quite articulate sentences kept coming out. I was embarrassed by my own foggy prejudice; and also, in the face of his extravagant self-assurance, cowed. I'm not surprised he doesn't remember.

And what John has to accept is that you can't help focusing on him – partly because he's too big a target to miss, partly because his work is so individual. For one thing, it packs a walloping "I." Even when a tale is ostensibly told by another – for example, the narrator of the kayaking story, "Requiem for Ronnie," or the old drunk who tells of a terrifying airborne rout from Jakarta – it's John talking. His trademark humor and flamboyance are overwhelming. Back in the 70s when John was the center of California rock climbing, everyone talked like him. Everyone was running around saying, "Ho, ma-an."

John has a compelling history, starting when he was one of this country's best rock climbers. He taught himself to climb in 1969, then quickly tried to teach everybody else so that he would have partners. He was very ambitious, and by 1972 was tearing up the local climbing standards. He completed hundreds of new routes, including the first 5.12 – on a scale of difficulty that then went from 5.0 to 5.12 – in California. He pushed standards in bouldering (practicing on rocks low to the ground, without rope), becoming known for his daring double-dynos, or two-handed lunges. He was also an iron rat – a weight-room fanatic – the first in his climbing gang to introduce heavy outside training into their sport.

John did things that would shape where climbing was going. In Yosemite in 1975, he and two friends, Billy Westbay and Jim Bridwell, were the first to climb one of the big routes on the 3000-foot El Capitan in a day. That same year, John was the guiding force on an ascent of the 1500-foot Yosemite route *Astroman* with John Bachar and Ron Kauk. The endlessly strenuous line became this country's premier long hard route, the one virtually all foreign climbers had heard of.

Over the years I read John's works more and more avidly. Some I loved, one I fervently hated, but they always got a rise out of me. They made me laugh out loud even if I was by myself.

"The Only Blasphemy," published in 1979, is probably still John's best-known piece. It has a great opening, with him racing across the desert at 85 mph on his way to Joshua Tree, thinking of a pal who'd recently fallen there while soloing (climbing ropeless). Next, John almost "decks out" himself while keeping up with that solo-master John Bachar. And the story has a great ending: all adding up to a quick, clean, exciting read. Moreover, the part where John extricates his fast-tiring self by saying, "At least die trying," became my own maxim on climbs. Not that I was soloing; but when I was flaming, about to drop, the phrase popped into my head. Out of control, I would flail upward, and sometimes grab a good hold.

By the late 70s John's interest in climbing was slacking off. And so Largo became Jungle John. In the early to mid-80s rumors came back: he was making a coast-to-coast crossing of Borneo, he'd found the largest underground cave in the world, he was in New Guinea among cannibals.

In fact, from 1979 to 84 John was mostly working for a biannual ABC special, David Frost's *International Guinness Book of World Records*, for which he was a cameraman and production coordinator. From that era he got much of his raw material – for "Auyan Tepui: A Fool's Pursuit," for example, about going to Venezuela to do the longest rappel in the world (and, naturally, getting lost in a helicopter in a typhoon), and "Down and Out," about filming the world's longest BASE jump in Norway. Other documentaries followed, and some location-scouting for the Disney Channel, from which came the exquisitely tension-filled "The Improbable Marksman." In that story John sloshes through the jungle in Sarawak with an Iban chief who is closely, mystifyingly tailed by a Malaysian soldier, gun poised, looking ready to blow the chief away at any second. Another adventure, the Borneo passage, was funded, fittingly, by Camel cigarettes. As a writer for *Outside* magazine put it, "Long is the genuine article, the guy in the Camel ad stepped off the page."

One day I got a letter from John, just a few lines, all caps, containing strong exhortations about my writing. "Cut loose," he ordered. "Forget journalism. Let's hear a blockbuster." It ended with "Chow! Largo." Thus began a very occasional correspondence.

John's prose is as muscular and vital as its source, full of such verbs as rocketing, scatting, zips, whop, shatters, claws, chewed, swills, and bonk; or phrases like "I rifled out," "arms shot, legs wobbling, head ablaze," "then I got maytagged around," and "whop! whop! whop!" The stories are mock-heroic, the pace is breakneck; it reels and careens. You could mark the margins of dozens of passages with "pure Largo." One such is in the absolutely wild "Tirada Los Tubos," where John and Luis, the macho brother of John's Venezuelan fianceé, go "tube shooting," jumping down the dark pipes that reroute local rivers. "No sound from the Indian," John remarks mid-shoot of a man ahead, whose necky example John and Luis had felt honor-bound to follow. "I flail for Luis Manuel and we lock arms, treading, terrified. We are whirling as in a draining bathtub, and when we're whisked into the eye we spin, gasp what I reckon are last breaths, and get sucked down a thin, black, vertical shaft. In two seconds – which last a century – we smack bottom and are gushed out into a larger pipe known to be so only by the more gentle curvature beneath my speeding tail. Wooo . . . . We skim down a ramp so steep my arms fly up, and we start racing anew, only slightly reassured by the stale air and the Indian's distant screams."

The flow of the dizzying style is so natural that I assumed it came readily. Surprisingly, John says, "It took me a long time to have any success at doing that. It's still hard. It's fatiguing."

Many of the works in this book have appeared before, in outdoor magazines such as *Climbing, Rock & Ice, Mountain,* and *Backpacker.* Three appeared in the literary journals *Tri-Quarterly* and *Plowshare.* But at least half are new.

In them, John tells some tall tales – whoppers – a part of the grand tradition of storytellers. Certainly he is the consummate entertainer. People who've been lucky enough to hear his readings still talk about them. He has been known to rouse everyone nearby, see to it that nobody was too straight or sober, and sweep around in an animated version of, for instance, "I Smoked Pipeloads with Bigfoot."

But these days John is moving away from his hareball adventure chronicles, feeling the style is inherently limited in its ability to touch the heart. He is aiming toward that higher level.

It follows that among John's favorite stories are "A Stone from Allah" and "Requiem for Ronnie," both intended to move, both told sadly. But those, perversely, are my least favorite. I crow over "Blasphemy" and "Tirada," which he dismisses, saying of the former, "For the life of me, I can't figure out why that's so popular. There's nothing there." We do, however, agree on the hyperkinetic "Dream On, Irian Jaya," the careful "Improbable Marksman," and "Down and Out," a moving characterization of the BASE jumper Carl Boenish, who talks non-stop about everything from hang-gliding and literature to mysticism, revelations and wacked-out medical theories. John's descriptions of this "bedeviled babbling" are affectionate, his account of Boenish's eventual fate restrained, lyrical, and heartfelt. "I didn't embellish that story," John told me. "I couldn't."

What writers have influenced him? In "Tirada" you will find a parody of Gabriel Garcia Marquez, in the phrasing, the click-snap-click-snap of the bugs, in a lunge for a cockroach. Other influences range from *Arabian Nights* to Joseph Conrad, Jim Harrison and Graham Greene. But John Long is an original. His voice is his own. His comical stuff is very much his own. "I am," he says, "a genetic buffoon."

Today John is a freelance script writer, living half in Hollywood and half in Venezuela with his wife, Mariana, and their baby daughter. "I'm not going to do entertainments anymore," he says, "but human short stories, not meant just to rivet and be fun." He relents. "There'll be *some* fun parts to them."

John is climbing again, although irregularly; a few years ago Charles Cole and some other friends dragged him back into it. Says Cole, "We couldn't stand not having him climb."

There's a duality in John. He is awfully good at being Largo. I can't exactly imagine him showing weakness, confessing to feeling a little down one day. He is the quintessential Largo in his hilarious rock climbing videos, wearing shades and playing the fool, calling his friend a knucklehead when it is he who has turned the rope into spaghetti. Or as the Indiana-Jones Largo, swimming to explore a pitch-black underground river, and smacking his head on a stalactite. I think John could become famous at being Largo.

But John is, in a way that is less sure than the usual Largo, reaching for something more. This is good. Just please don't leave Largo behind. We couldn't stand not having him.

ALISON OSIUS
Climbing Magazine

Aspen
January, 1989

The little bush plane was horse-shoed around a good-sized banyan, and we thought it a miracle that anyone could have survived.

"I've never seen anything like it," the young pilot started. "It came on like gorilla monsoon . . . ."

Juan Domingo Bustos
JUNGLE PILOTS

Contents

Tirada *Los Tubos*

I HAD PACKED UP and headed back to Venezuela. Solomon's Army couldn't handle the work I had a month to finish, but I went anyway. Mariana could flee her teaching job in a phoneless jungle for a week to visit friends and family in El Tigre, her home town. If I didn't join her, brother Luis Manuel would pistol whip me on my next visit.

We meet in Maracaibo and head to El Tigre, a blistering savannah peppered with galloping oil rigs. Many gringo engineers hole up here in vast and hermetically sealed campamientos which they never leave except to go to the airport. The tangy taste of salsa and the tropical smell of mango hang thick in the air; eyes squint, nostrils flare, mouths water, ears duck the tic-snap-tic-snap of the big bugs, never seen, but most assuredly here. The mercury sizzles at ninety-seven, humidity likewise.

The cement shack goes wild when we arrive. Three-hundred-pound Grandmama stops kneading the torta and tremors to her feet. Sister Estella, squat and jolly, trots forth with all manner of greasy foods. Kids jump from shady nooks while Luis Manuel swarms from his hammock into his room. He emerges whooping as a gaucho, wearing a cowboy hat and waving a long-barreled pistola, bursting past us and into the yard to fire three glorious rounds into the sky. In gleeful song, he lays down a few

Venezolano dance steps, boots a sleeping dog, cracks his bullwhip, fires a fourth shot into a stump, then slaps my back until
I'm gasping. Ten chickens take cackling flight. A frightened
turkey flares its plumage. The dog is gone. A thick-necked, bull-
working stud, Luis Manuel is the quintessence of machismo.
Sweat pours down his unshaven face and, of course, he has a
mustache. When his black eyes needle down, I know what will
follow: Matrimonio? Cuando? When a *very* tentative date is
suggested, Estella swoons and Luis Manuel's eyes fire like
cannons. He kisses me, then Mariana, then Grandmama, then
Estella, then me, breaking into ludicrous lyric, more dance moves,
faster this time. He then makes for his pistola to halt at a bottle
of Ron Añejo, proffered in Grandmama's plump and stingy
hands. He swills a tan inch and carries on, bottle up, till Estella
rips it free for Grandmama to lock in a cupboard to which there
is one key only; this rests in Grandmama's brassiere, a fallow
acre no man sober or drunk should trespass. Food is taken, drink
is taken. As sure as night, boredom descends. Click-snap- click-
snap.

Luis Manuel is all energy, impatience, daring. El Tigre is dead,
so he is ever contriving excitement through motorcycling and the
like. He's got a plan, he's always got a plan; he paces like a
maniac. More than once I've feared for my life, joining Luis
Manuel's shenanigans. (Most memorable was bulldogging range
donkeys, a stunt that cost Luis Manuel several teeth and a
fractured collarbone.) His enthusiasm suggests that this time I'm
really in for it: "Tirada los tubos!" Grandmama balks; her hands
shoot up and she giggles like a great tub of Jello. Tube shooting?
Si, senor! Luis is rapt, leans in for impact. It comes down near
Tascabana, thirty miles out of town. During construction of the
nearly completed hydro-electric plant, the Cariña Indians had
discovered tube shooting through drunken accident. The plant's
cooling system required re-routing all the surrounding rivers; this
was accomplished with three-foot steel tubes that piped the
water a meandering route to a central aqueduct. "Tirada los
tubos" is simple: one enters a tube half full of water, becoming
a human torpedo, speeding in black, downhill passage for
hundreds of yards to a free-fall exit into the aqueduct, deep and
calm. This sounds like a Grand Prix version of the "water rides"

D.B. and I had spent a day rocketing down in an Australian amusement park. Whatever, it certainly sounds superior to sweltering away the day at the desk.

Rapt with anticipation, Luis Manuel illustrates by assuming various dive-bomb positions on the floor until he spots a terrific cucaracha on yonder wall – a three incher, black as an E-flat piano key. He springs for his bullwhip but is brained in mid-stride by Estella's cane. The roach zips into a chink beyond the lunging boys, and we're all laughs, particularly Grandmama, who then farts like a tent ripping. As she continues howling, the key clinks from her dress. Luis Manuel dives, but gets only a handful of Estella's shoe. Grandmama repositions the key, then again breaks wind; so we've just got to get outside.

Luis Manuel fans his torso with his hat and with a tragic face pines the fact that tomorrow will mark the end of tube shooting. Grates will be welded over the tube's entrances, for when the plant fires up on Sunday, the water will rise to pipe-bursting proportions. Luis Manuel mops his forehead, then spits for effect. The chickens are roosting. The turkey's in the oven. The dog's in Ecuador and he's out of beer, so there's nothing to be done but grab his bullwhip and look for cockroaches. CRACK!

Luis Manuel did say the tubes were no secret, but his inch is close to a yard, so I'm blown away by the mob we join at Tascabana. According to Luis Manuel, it's the social event of the decade. Some have driven from as far away as Ciudad Bolivar, nothing compared to the Indians who had punished their burros upwards of two days across torrid, brick-hard plains to shoot the tubes, or drink, or both. The City Council had created various safety procedures, with the military dispatching a phalanx of soldiers to enforce them. As we close in on the circus, it becomes all the more sprawling. From atop cars sunk into opposite banks of an Olympic-sized mudhole, the Mayor and one Colonel Juan de Jesus Aquilla Montearoya megaphone orders, which sound like so much white noise when challenged by the distorted stereos of five hundred cars girding the sump in a formation so tight that one treads trunk, roof, then hoods just to gain the tubes. At the waterline, purveyors ply the mud with fried pig fat and bottled pop, and already the pool is awash in trash equaling that of a World Cup soccer match. Hundreds laugh, push, jeer, and shout, but everyone's so antsy to go that both trash and humans rapidly drain down twenty odd tubes. Tube shooters are continuously replaced by roof hoppers on the rebound, ecstatic smiles stretching their faces. The whole commotion is one churning riot of white-hot Latin fun. But Luis Manuel is suspicious of a curious layer of foam in the water and will have none of this commoners' pool. We head for a higher pool entry featuring longer, faster, more dangerous tubes.

One-half mile north, a second mudhole shows one-tenth the crowd, half the tubes, and five times the soldiers. I'm trembling when I dive and stroke for a tube, but – Alto! A soldier must first take an "official" ride. "Porque?" begs Luis Manuel. "El gordo, El gordo," laughs an armed private. The scout departs feet first, ostensibly to flush the tube.

I grab Luis Manuel's feet and we slip in head first. The turns are not smooth and sweeping, rather ten- to twenty-degree welded elbows, so at turn one we're jolted apart, as are half my vertebrae and most of my teeth. Due to constant water flow, the tubes are well mossed – Hail Mary, lest the sides strip my flesh to the bone. Now I'm vaulting faster than I ever imagined. Bang! I slam through another turn. It's pitch dark, so the apprehension of the next elbow keeps my arms extended while my heart races. wooosh! The farther I go, the greater the speed, and if a sharp turn is ahead, I'll dent the tube. Screams and careening bodies echo about. After a long minute and hundreds of yards, just as my stomach turns in terror, light shows far ahead; I approach like a bullet and pop! I rifle out and free-fall into casual water, hoping not to bonk heads with some dawdler. I doubt most would have braved the tubes had they known of the blistering speed or slamming turns, but one foot in and it's too late, and few regret it after the fact. Rubbing bruised shoulders and hips, I swim through the crowd to survey the exit from afar.

A fifty-foot cement wall is festooned with over a hundred pissing tubes, whose positions vary from below the water to above the cement. From the profusion of tubes, I'm assured of Luis Manuel's claim that all pipes terminate here, laying to rest my fear of some odd pipe spitting me out in Paraguay. It's hilarious to see the screaming bodies come whistling forth, backward, upside down, limbs akimbo, landing on friends who have landed on friends. The stunned, dumbfounded riders hobble to the bank, crossing themselves and rubbing their contusions. One ride is more than ample for most, but the durable and game can't seem to get enough. But everyone pauses to breathe, count licks.

Sometime after the fifth or sixth ride, I'm massaging my bruised shoulders and see a crazed Indian come rocketing out at the forty-five foot level, limbs flailing, voice wailing, while all below him dive for cover. By the distance he clears the pipe, it's obvious he has found that tube which launches the human torpedo. Whop! He belly flops, yet quickly swims to the bank, apparently unscathed. He races off without a backward glance. Luis Manuel looks angry to have been outdone, so we scamper after the Indian. Fortunately, we lose him in the crowd.

Plodding on, I notice steady traffic wavering to and from a cordoned area. Luis Manuel explains. Drinking is strictly forbidden anywhere near the tubes, but anyone willing to hike the 125 yards to this huddle can drink himself half dead and straightaway return to the pipes.

Back at our mudhole, Luis Manuel spots some muddy footprints leading off. We track them a quarter mile to a knee-deep rivulet that is vacant save for that Indian we just saw delivered forty- five feet above the Río San Tome. Luis Manuel beams. With indecision, the Indian variously checks five half-submerged tubes. Luis Manuel says it hardly matters since all pipes lead to Rome. When I note that these pipes appear quite a bit older than the former ones, corroded and rusty, Luis Manuel explains that many of the pipes were old and rusty when first installed. I question the Indian, who replies by diving headfirst into the middle pipe.

I'll take this one in the luge position, thinking that if the pipe should take a drastic crook, my feet, rather than mi cabeza, will absorb the impact. This proves wise since after ten seconds the pipe angles sharply. Luis Manuel – head first and two seconds ahead – screams from reflex as we accelerate God awfully. Then, bam! Ay, mi glutio, the pipe having leveled before dropping even sharper. Now I'm going so fast that touching the side feels like dragging a hand on an expressway. I blindly try to stay centered on the slime, clutching my gonads, praying there will be no U-turns or sloppy welds. The Indian's echo recedes to nothing. Then: AYEEEE . . . . There's no pipe beneath us! It's a hideous sensation tumbling through darkness ten, twenty, thirty feet to splash into some sort of tank. No sound from the Indian. I flail for Luis Manuel and we lock arms, treading, terrified. We are whirling as in a draining bathtub, and when we're whisked into the eye we spin, gasp what I reckon are last breaths, and get sucked down a thin, black, vertical shaft. In two seconds – which last a century – we smack bottom and are gushed out into a larger pipe known to be so only by the more gentle curvature beneath my speeding tail. woooo . . . . We skim down a ramp so steep my arms fly up, and we start racing anew, only slightly reassured by the stale air and the Indian's distant screams. These shortly give way to something sounding like a drumstick raked across a mile-long charrasca. We in turn grind into a corrugated stretch that sets limbs flying like a ragdoll's, tweaking and wrenching every joint. Then I slam into an elbow, which knocks me senseless; I see stars despite total darkness. The aqueduct is way behind us. There's no screaming now. I'm rocked half stupid, whistle along for several straight miles, and regain some sense, but loads more fear. Finally I manage a scream, as does Luis Manuel, somewhere behind. We're helpless but to course through the darkness. We bruise off a final bend and whip toward a pinhole of light well ahead, looking like the Sacred Virgin herself. I breathe again, then bash across a final washboard, only partially acknowledging a fifteen-foot free-fall into more mud than water.

This ordeal has taken somewhere between six and eight minutes. The mud is dry before I can rise, dazed, feeling like I've tumbled off a speeding melon truck. I wobble toward moving water to soak and check my injuries. The Indian and Luis Manuel are moaning horribly. The Indian has a strained neck, can't move his head; Luis Manuel rubs his collarbone as blood flows freely from a nasty gash above his eye. We all have ruby-red bash marks, everywhere. My hips and elbows barely work; my hams are like ripe tomatoes, but nothing's broken and I'm okay if I don't move. The distant sound of trucks marks the highway two miles off. It's not a great distance, though we'll be hoofing it naked since the tubes have stripped the trunks off all three of us.

Requiem for Ronnie

THE FOLLOWING EPIC was told to me recently in Malibu, California. I have changed the names and any details that might place the narrator – a close friend – in a bind. A judge might fault him, though he could never deny his strict duress, nor his humane treatment of a friend. Here, then, is his story.

•

Hank and I worked in an office so large I never really knew what he did. I did little of consequence; the boss kept me on only because I'd been an Olympian. I was busy poring over a photo of my recent jaunt down the Bio Bio River in Chile when Hank came over to my desk.

"Do a little paddling, boy?"

"A little." The entire office knew me as "the paddling fool." Hank snatched the photo from my hands, took a glance, then flipped it back on the desk.

"Nice little creek."

"That's strictly world class, my friend."

"Kid stuff," Hank replied. "Bet you think you're pretty good."

"I've got more experience on big rivers than any man alive," I said, comically expanding my chest.

"Anyone but me," Hank corrected. I laughed at that one. Hank did not.

"Bullshit!" I cracked.

Hank leaned in close. "I can paddle circles around you and anyone you've ever seen."

Mind you, this had all been friendly banter, but now I had to call Hank's bluff. A paddler's experience is told in his hands, and I grabbed Hank's. He allowed me a two-second glance before retracting them. I was shocked. Those were not office hands, but the hands of a galley slave.

"I need a partner for something. Not this kind of fluff," Hank said, pointing to me cresting a spuming 20-foot swell, "but a real river. You interested?"

"Sure," I stuttered, thinking this was all a joke. Hank scribbled his address on a note pad.

"Just kidding about the Bio Bio, but I'd like to talk things over tonight. Can you make it?"

"Count on it!"

As I barreled out of town that night, my head swam in confusion. First, there were those horrendous hands. Second, why would a fellow paddler hide from me for two years? Maybe he wasn't a paddler. Maybe he chopped wood all night. Hank lived way out of town, and he answered the door wearing only gym trunks, his body glistening with perspiration and fiberglass dust. His torso looked chiseled from white marble.

"Just patching up a boat. Come on in and grab a beer." His house was not a home, but rather a warehouse of kayaks, paint, resin, and float bags. Every room was a workshop, save the one decked in topographic maps and photos. I grabbed a beer and Hank showed me some of his boats. Most were weird, experimental designs, and each bore a little drawing that I thought was some kind of Indian motif, though I didn't ask. My eyes ran from the resin fumes. We had hardly settled into the chart room when Hank grew real intense, and his next remark made me think the fumes had taken hold.

"Look here, Lance, can you paddle the desperate stuff or not? And be honest, or it may cost you your life." My life? I was sick of all this intrigue.

"What are you getting at?" I started. "And who the hell are you to question my abilities?"

"I'm not talking about running gates. I'm talking about wild rivers. I don't want to get you killed, that's all."

"I don't plan to let you, Hank."

"Good," Hank smiled. "I tried to run the Rio Juarez last weekend, but it was a bit much to run alone. If you'll join me on another attempt, I'll pay for the helicopter and all that." I'd never seen the Rio Juarez, but those who had agreed it was suicidal.

"I'll look at it."

"Oh, it's perfectly runnable," Hank assured me, "but not solo."

"As I said, I'll take a look."

"Great," Hank stated, "but if we're going to paddle together, you've got to play by my rules."

"Rules?"

"This may sound ridiculous, but you can never mention any of our runs to anybody. It's all been a game with me – paddling alone, just keeping to myself. That's why I've never had you over till now; and now I need you." Hank chuckled with a start. "Maybe I'll explain it to you later, but for now, if you'll swear to secrecy, you will soon be running rapids you never thought even remotely possible; but I can't promise that you'll live long enough to take credit for them." I leaped up and started pacing the room. I was the acknowledged big-water kingpin, and hearing this kind of talk caught me totally off balance.

"You know, the Rio Juarez is universally recognized as lethal," I quipped.

"We'll be the judge of that," barked Hank. "Are we on, or not?" Hank's eyes burned.

"Really, Hank, I've never seen you paddle an inch. We'll do a warm-up first, then go from there."

"Fair enough."

"How about the Tuolumne?"

"That rivulet?!" Hank laughed. Next day we both called in sick and were on the water before noon.

A week of Sierra storms had drained into the Tuolumne, and treacherous high water raged west into the San Joaquin Valley. As we struggled into wetsuits, I told Hank he'd better be the ace he claimed or he'd be paddling through the pearly gates in about one hundred yards. He laughed in my face, then cranked out into the stout current. I fell in behind. In the next quarter mile, I saw that Hank was a superlative paddler. After another quarter mile I realized he was peerless. Then he cut loose. He would slalom through jagged wash rocks, then bow forward, plunging the nose of his kayak in a wave. His boat would pop straight up and flop endwise into the eye of a boiling vortex, where he'd loop around, and fire out downstream – underwater. He'd crab his boat sideways through steaming rapids, logrolling, over and over. And he ran an entire stretch backward! Here I was just trying to survive, while Hank toyed with rapids that had killed more than one expert. I had never seen anything like it – not even close – and I had seen every world champion of the last eight years. Hank never stopped for a break or scouted ahead, lest we "rob the creek of the small challenge it could offer." Consequently, we powered through a normal day's run in four hours.

On the drive home, I was so flabbergasted that I hardly knew where to start or what questions to ask. Had Hank been my equal, or even a little better, my ego would have struggled with this, but he was so far beyond me that it seemed almost comical. No one could get that good on their own, paddling in a vacuum.

"So who did you compete for, Hank?"

"Never did."

"Well, what other great paddlers have you run with?"

"Only you." I was at once charmed and frustrated.

"Come on, Hank, what's with the secret agent stuff?" Hank immediately grew intense.

"We had an agreement. We're going to paddle together, and that's it. We shook on that, remember?" All this stealth seemed absurd, but I didn't press it. "That's good enough for me, Hank. But if you just saw a guy long jump the Grand Canyon, you'd be curious, believe me." Hank smiled slightly.

Four months passed before the Rio Juarez came into form, and we were plenty active in the meantime. We hit a score of furious rapids, or "rooks," as Hank called them: the Moyle; the Kayan; the Coruh in flood. I learned that much of Hank's wizardry lay in his confidence to try anything. With his coaxing, I too started charging into fuming geysers and hydraulics, rarely opting for sane water on the the flanks. The idea was to challenge the river.

After a dozen outings I had picked up several of Hank's stunts, though to a far lesser degree; but I could never fathom running class 6 rapids backward. On the water, we were fast pals, but off it Hank was paranoid in guarding the smallest detail of his personal life, and there was a marked tension between us. The few times we encountered other paddlers, Hank took ridiculous measures to avoid even eye contact – yanking his boat into the shrubs, or holing up for hours to avoid passing a camp in daylight. Once we even paddled the Salmon by moonlight! But even this vexed me less than his divine talent. He *had* to have competed at some time. Or some notable had at least seen or heard about him. I called my old coach, Dan Lamay.

"Dan, have you ever heard of a paddler named Hank Crawford?"

"Don't think so . . . ."

"Yeah, I figured as much. Look, I've been paddling with a guy who is twice as good as anybody you've ever seen. Do you remember any phenoms from way back – this guy's probably in his mid- thirties, at least."

"Well, there were standouts, but not like you're talking about. Anyway, you saw all those guys: Mittan, Gerwald, Ronson . . . ." We talked about other things, like Dan's current Olympic team, and just as I was accepting that Hank had actually sprung from the blue, Dan chimed back in.

"You know, before old Finnegan quit coaching, he used to talk about a kid named Hard, or Hearth, or something like that. He was only with the team a short while before he got thrown in jail. I do know he raced against Gerwald once and beat him pretty handily."

"He beat Gerwald?" Gerwald was a legendary, six-time world champ. "Supposedly, he crushed him, but I don't know. That had to be fifteen years ago, at least, and I wasn't there."

It took me two days to track down Finnegan, who was living with a daughter in Wyoming. His voice was breathy and labored.

"Heart. His name was Ronnie Heart," the old coach corrected. "He was with the team only long enough to compete in one international meet, which he won by over twenty seconds. They thought he ran an illegal boat, or was on amphetamines, and so on. Nobody thought an unknown could crush the world's best, but Heart did – easily. But I'll tell you, as good as he was running gates, his real genius was in big white water. We'd take training runs down the Snake and Tuolumne, and Heart was absolutely magic. He'd run entire sections backward."

"So where is he, coach?" There was a long pause.

"Oh, he's dead now. Died fighting fires in Sequoia. He was a little wild, Heart was, and he got in a car accident that killed everyone but him. The judge found him negligent and sentenced him hard – like fifteen years. You know they have convicts fighting fires these days. Heart and a couple of others got caught on a ridge; the few remains they found were even beyond the experts to sort out." I smiled.

"One last thing, coach. Did this Heart use any weird gear?"

"And how. He'd run these homemade jobs all painted up with Navajo designs. You know, he grew up in Navajoland, just outside of Lee's Ferry, on the Colorado River."

"Probably ran the Grand Canyon a lot, eh?"

"Something like 200 times before he was sixteen. The sad part is, he was only nineteen when he died. No one will ever know how great he might have become." Nobody but me, I thought. Whether Finnegan and Heart shared a confidence is something I often pondered but never determined, since the old man fell to leukemia soon thereafter.

Several days later, Hank and I spread out the charts and started reviewing the topography we had memorized months before. A thick black line, the Rio Juarez, snaked through the contours passing numerous mentions of the phrase Piedra Caliza – limestone. There was no nearby road access, so we – or rather Hank – would have to charter a helicopter in Laredo. The river was in Mexico, whose air space required all kinds of impossible permits. The pilot would drop us at the mouth of the canyon, just over the border, but he'd go no further. That meant running the river sight unseen. The charts showed no waterfalls, anyway. Hank heaved a sigh.

"Good thing we're honed up. This is going to test us," Hank promised, tapping the circuitous black line with his finger. Hank's hand came up to his forehead, and he stared hard at nothing.

"How you feeling, Lance . . . any second thoughts?"

"No way!" I assured him, privately trembling. Clearly, he didn't want his passion to color my decision; or simply, he didn't want me dying at his design. I wondered if all this was not a spill-over from that tragic accident of so many years ago. And how many had died? And who were they – family, hitch-hikers, Navajos? I'd never know. I wanted to lift the veil, to disclose my talk with Finnegan, but the timing was off. The hour would come, I was certain.

We went for it the following Saturday. From a nearby sand bar the river's howl drowned the whomp-whomp of the receeding chopper. At the first sight of the river, my heart leapt into my mouth. A terrible sluice, the torrent rip-roared directly into the gorge before hooking left and disappearing. For five minutes we just stared. I didn't know water could move that fast. An occasional uprooted oak would tear by, barely holding its own above the frothy surface. I kept pushing down the notion of a bushwhack to the nearest farm road, which we knew was ten miles east.

"Looks like a big sled ride," said Hank, studying the flow.

"Should be okay if we stay centered in the current," I lied. Four months back, I wouldn't have entered that river under a trained cannon. We had no idea what lay a quarter mile downstream. Hank shoved his boat to the water line and got in.

"Pull over whenever you can," Hank said, eyes riveted ahead. "We've got to scout this one real good." I nodded, cinching my helmet till my teeth locked. We shoved off together. Hank took a couple deep strokes, and I fell in behind him. When we entered the current, my head snapped back from the speed. Right off I went over, but rolled up okay. We barreled on, knifing through huge rooster tails of white water, constantly leaning, bracing, trying to follow the central flow. The river churned so much that the top few feet were foam, so we moved principally on feel. The current eased as we entered the actual gorge, limestone slabs ambling up from the water line. Then we heard it, around the corner: a low rumbling reverberating about the narrow canyon walls.

"Get left!" shrieked Hank, paddling hard across the strong current, his boat lunging with each stroke. No eddies meant no stopping. We turned the corner with our shoulders nearly brushing the left wall. Just ahead, the entire left side'of the river spun into a colossal whirlpool, the very edge of which swirled clockwise up and off the wall. A halo of mist revolved around the maw, which gained in size and fury the closer we got. It had to be fifty feet across. No question, we were headed for a "keeper" hole.

"Hug the cliff!" Hank screamed. Our one chance lay in riding the left-hand lip of the whirlpool, using its downstream momentum to spin us past the hole. Feeling the circular current tugging me right, I dug my paddle deep left. My boat jumped straight and I caught the surge flowing off the wall. The force rolled me on edge, the bottom of my boat grinding across the limestone. The mist blinded me, but for one split second the halo parted, and I gaped straight into the swirling gullet, the home of great and grinding boulders. Just when I thought I might tumble into it, my boat slipped down off the wall and I caught the downstream edge of the whirlpool. My bow shot up under the cross current, and I felt it drawing me back in. I briefly teetered, dead in the water, rocking on the very brink; and only a few atomic strokes vaulted me onto the calm.

I screamed until the limestone walls trembled, then paddled over to Hank. A diabolical smile stretched across his face.

"Buckle up, boy, we're heading for the real McCoy!"

Shortly, the river screamed through two walls of living rock which reared vertically off the water. In spite of our breakneck speed, the going was now smooth, and we covered about fifteen miles in the next hour. Twice the river pinched to culvert-size and passed beneath natural bridges; the ceiling on one was but a body length above us. Then the river angled sharply, rifling us through a slalom course of rock pinnacles sprouting from the water like great ten-pins on end. On each side of these leapt diamond wakes the breadth of a speed boat, requiring all my expertise running gates to avoid them. Twice they flipped me and twice I had to paddle rabidly to avoid a fatal head on. Impacting a pinnacle might not have killed me outright, but it would have demolished the boat, without which I would have drowned in a heartbeat. There was no shore to grope for, no alcove to hide in. When we finally pulled into calm waters, we had been toiling full bore for over two hours. We made for a thank-God shelf out left, dragged our boats onto it, and collapsed. My hands were cramping badly. Hank had smacked the canyon wall, which cost him the left arm of his wetsuit and gave him a nasty rake across the forearm. I must have struck some debris, because my boat leaked slightly. We were inextricably committed, fighting to survive. One glance downstream said our chances were slim or none.

One hundred feet below, the river pitched and accelerated into a boiling rage that seemed too ferocious for mere limestone to contain. Fifty feet further, the canyon pinched before hooking left. At the elbow the entire river dashed forty feet up the right wall in a seething, perpetual wave. What loomed around the corner seemed immaterial.

"Look at that!" yelled Hank. A huge pine log torpedoed past. Bald from its long passage, it looked like a great sausage bobbing atop the whitewater. It disappeared, then popped up just before the elbow. My stomach turned as it arced thirty feet up and sixty feet across the face of the perpetual wave. At the wave's apex, it tumbled down, end over end, and was washed around the corner.

"We can make this," cried Hank. "The water's so high that it should flush us out so long as we stay centered in the current. We've got to set up to come in low on that wave, though." Hank cinched the strap on his helmet and started for his boat. "Let's go, Lance. It's no good staring at it."

But I couldn't move, nor could I fathom Hank's readiness to tackle something combining a forty-foot Makaha wave with a section of Niagara Falls – though we had no choice. It wasn't courageous paddling into this, I thought, because there was no way to survive it. Hank grabbed my arm and smiled.

"Hey, you don't think I'm scared? Why do you think I brought you along? To share the terror, man! Dig in, Lance, we're going to make this!" And you know, I believed him.

We paddled over to the far right. The rumble was deafening. Vaulting toward the bend, I saw that Hank – just ahead – came in too high as he charged onto the perpetual wave. He sliced across, then zoomed almost straight up to the crest. He dug his right paddle, the end of his boat slid around, and he shot down the wave – backward, but perfectly aligned. Facing me, Hank plunged off the wave and into the cataract before me, a devil-may-care smile all over his face. And even above the roar, I heard him yell: "It's the real McCoy!" Then I too dove into the falls and was swallowed. Locked inside the plunging tube, I fell, fell. The impact instantly stripped me of boat, and the falls drove me to the bottom and pinned me there, face down. Then I got maytaged around, feeling as though my limbs would be ripped apart. I surfaced facing the falls, where wakes swamped me over and over. Without a life jacket, I would certainly have drowned. Limp and gasping, I bobbed into calm waters. I spotted Hank downstream, an arm drapped over each boat. Retching up half the river, his hacking soon turned into a howl.

"We've done it. That's the real McCoy, Lance. We've done the real McCoy." I struggled over to the boats, draped my arms over the bow, and blew about a pint of water out of my sineses.

"I defy you to find a tougher run," Hank wailed.

"I don't want to," I gasped.

"That's it. The ultimate – no one can top it," he rambled on.

"I'll never try, I promise you."

"And you took the easy way."

"You didn't . . . ." But Hank's smile assured me he had done the doubly unthinkable, that he'd intentionally lined up high on the wave and had taken on the falls – backward. The falls had finally stripped his paranoia and laid bare the real man – a kid who'd found the golden egg. Hank ranted on.

We kicked over to the narrow shore, dumped the water from our boats, and lay back. The boats had taken a thrashing, and I noted the last run had ground the little Navajo design right off Hank's boat. No matter. Hank kept blabbering and slapping my back and carrying on in a manner I would have thought impossible thirty minutes before. The ice man had melted. I was tempted to reveal my secret, but he so enjoyed himself that I didn't want to risk spoiling the moment. Until then, the full measure of our luck had not come home to us, preoccupied as we'd been with survival. But now an ecstatic release came over me. No question: I'd cheated death. Though the soggy map showed more limestone ahead, we had quit the narrowest canyon, and by all indications had only twenty miles of easier river to reach Los Estribos, a town of 9,000.

We had planned on two days, but it was only mid-afternoon, so, at Hank's urging, we pushed on. I felt half dead, but snapped to at the first white water, where Hank clowned through fifteen-foot swells. The guy was in heaven.

Then the river unexpectedly dropped, charging on with the same gusto it had above the falls. We cranked around a bend, where just before us, the entire river flowed straight into a mountainside. Of course it went under this buttress, but the only visible breach was a tiny chink dead center, looking like a doghouse door as we hurtled toward it. This all happened faster than I could panic, and I reflexively lined up behind Hank. Twenty feet before the wall, I saw the chink was sufficiently wide, but would clip our heads off unless . . . . I saw Hank flip upside down and knife into the crack just as I rolled over. Blazing down a swift river, upside down, inside a mountain, is a sensation I won't try to describe; and for fear of losing my head, I stayed upside down until my lungs felt to burst. I rolled up only to carom off the wall and plunge down again. Whatever I hit demolished my boat and pitched me head over heels through the darkness. Utterly stunned, I realized nothing until getting belched out of the mountain into calm but swift-moving water.

Fragments of our smashed boats floated around me. Miraculously, I was unhurt, still clutching my unbroken paddle. Beyond me, the river crept through open savannah. The canyon was definitely behind us now. But where was Hank? Then I spotted him, floating by the right bank. He didn't move as I stroked over to him. He was conscious, though dazed, as I dragged him onto the shore. I felt around for broken bones, and when I rolled him over, I nearly puked. Two daggers of fiberglass were sunk into his back. I drew out the first, perhaps four inches long, directly from his spine. When I removed an even bigger one from his side, a stream of blood gushed out and all my attempts to stop it were useless. No doubt about it, this guy was going to die on me then and there. I finally dragged him onto a little rock bench and sat him upright. Only then did I see that blood from a head gash had drained into his eyes. "Can you get my eyes? I can't move my arms," Hank asked calmly. He looked pale. I wiped his brow.

"Hank, you've got some deep wounds in your back, but we'll just rest up a while and take it from there."

"I'm history, Lance. I can't even feel my body." I couldn't say anything, and I must have looked terrified. "Relax," he reassured me. I couldn't look at him just then. When I could, he smiled wide.

"Thanks for paddling with me, Lance. These last few months have been terrific. You're the finest paddler I've ever seen."

"I'm nothing compared to you, Mr. Ronnie Heart." He coughed out a chuckle.

"I called old Finnegan and he told me everything. Even how you crushed Gerwald in Norway."

"That hack? He couldn't paddle a lick." I choked back my emotion.

"Ronnie, you could have been the world's champ for twenty years, easy."

"God, it sounds good to hear my name." His eyes misted over. "I never cared about running gates in some tank. That's not kayaking. What matters is big white water, and we ran the biggest."

"Ronnie, nobody will ever repeat what we've done – ever."

"I won't say never, but we were first."

"You were first, Ronnie. I always followed your lead."

We talked quietly for another ten minutes. I promised to keep Ronnie's secret, and to bury him right next to the river. His voice waned to a whisper, and though he couldn't raise an arm, his courage never flagged. "I could live another thousand years and never have a better day." Smiling slightly, he floated away, listening to the purling current that meant everything to him. It all happened so fast.

I now faced the hardest task of my life. I broke my paddle in half and used it to dig into the moist soil. In an hour, I laid the great Ronnie Heart to rest, where his soul could hear the rapids as long as the river flowed. As I heaped the ground upon him, I cried like a fool. I tried to say something pious, but it sounded so extraneous I quit. Can you really pity someone who died doing exactly as he pleased? I threw the broken paddles in the river and watched them drift into the night. I had nothing left – the river took it all.

The book had slammed shut on Ronnie Heart, and if this story were mere fiction, the fitting end was right there, on the river. Unfortunately, I still had to get off the river and out of Mexico. I collapsed on shore that night, watched a cold moon inch across the sky, and arose battered, stiff, and exhausted. I was starving. I took a compass bearing due east and set off, hoping to gain that farm road in half a day, terrain permitting. It didn't. After cresting a hill, the wet dirt turned to mud, ankle deep for a mile, then knee deep for two more. I had to plow a trough through the ooze. The sun beat down hard, and I kept thinking the mud would turn to quicksand. About noon, the mud gave way to waist-high thicket, each branch bristling with hooked thorns. No use trying to avoid the barbs, since getting free from one meant getting snagged by another. In ten minutes thorns were tearing straight through my wetsuit and into my flesh. Soon the shrub grew so thick that I had drag myself over the top on all fours. Branches snapped, dropping me into thorns which slashed my face and arms. My wetsuit hung in bloody tatters. I was so weary I could barely focus on my compass. Every time I tried to move on hunch, I found myself going awry. Hours later I stumbled upon a stagnant creek. I was too exhausted to continue, or even move, but the bugs were fearsome and swarmed about my wounds. To escape them, I groveled into the black water, set my head on the rocky bank, and passed out. By morning, the mosquitos had nearly closed both my eyes.

I pushed on, weak and stumbling. The ground was riven with little trenches which I would tumble into and exhaust myself trying to claw out of. My throut burned, and it took everything I had to read the compass: I would close my eyes, concentrate, then quickly glance before the needle would fuzz and dance. I later entered a half-mile stretch of putrid quagmires, passed by half swimming, half fording through the thick green soup. Every time I touched a log I thought it was a crocodile or something worse, and I struck out with fresh vigor. The final bog ended at a clay bank; with every effort to climb out the lip mushed away, pitching me back into the mire. The reeking water felt like acid on my wounds.

I gave up many times.

On flat ground at last, I crawled under a tree and lay breathless in meager shade. Voices came from nearby, and I looked up and saw – or thought I saw – two men on mules; but I was too spent to hail them. I must have swooned. When I came out of it, I spent my last energies crawling over to the road, maybe fifty yards. Of the next few hours I remember only fragments: a sunset, an oxcart, a bumpy ride, and a candle flickering in an adobe hovel.

I came around to find a wizened old Indian woman, digging thorns from my nakedness with a dull pin. An old man handed me a wineskin of water that I quaffed in one long draw. My hands were so torn and swollen I couldn't have even held a kayak paddle – as if I wanted to! I spent the next day dozing and eating while the old woman applied poultices to my wounds. I never understood a thing she or the old man said, so I couldn't convey my nightmare. Maybe that was better, since from then on, Ronnie's death was strictly my own affair. On the following day they hitched up the cart and took me to a highway near the border. I've always meant to go back and thank them. Maybe someday I will.

The Only Blasphemy

Whoso endangereth his days, e'en he 'scape deserveth no praise
ARABIAN NIGHTS

AT SPEEDS BEYOND 80 MPH the California cops jail you. I set out at 79. Tobin Sorenson drove 100 – did so until his Datsun blew. Tobin never drew the line. He had both reckless enthusiasm and a boundless fear threshold, and these, naturally, enamored him of soloing. It came as no surprise when he perished attempting to solo the north face of Mt. Alberta.

I charge toward Joshua Tree National Monument, where, two weeks previously, another pal had pitched while soloing. I later inspected the base of the route, wincing at the grisly blood stains, the tufts of matted hair. Soloing is unforgiving, but okay, I think. You just have to be realistic, not some fool abetted by peer pressure or ego. At 85, Joshua Tree comes quickly, but the stark night drags.

The morning sun peers over the flat horizon, gilding the rocks that spot the desert carpet. The biggest stones are little more than 150 feet high. I hook up with John Bachar, presently the world's foremost free climber. John abides at those climbing areas featuring the most sun. He has been at Joshua for two months and his soloing feats astonish everyone. It is winter, when school limits my climbing to weekends, so my motivation is there, but my fitness is not. Straightaway, Bachar suggests a "Half Dome day." Half Dome is 2,000 feet high, or 20 rope lengths. Hence, we must climb 20 pitches to get our Half Dome day. In a wink Bachar is shod, and cinching the sling on his chalk bag. "Ready?" Only now do I realize he intends to climb all 2,000 feet solo, without the safety of a rope. To save face, I agree, thinking: "Well, if he suggests something too asinine, I'll just draw the line. I was the first to start soloing in Joshua, anyhow . . . ."

We embark on vertical rock, twisting feet and jamming hands into bulging cracks; smearing the toes of skin-tight boots onto tenuous bumps; pulling over roofs on bulbous holds; palming off rough rock and marveling at it all. A little voice sometimes asks me how good a flexing, quarter-inch hold can be. If you're tight, you set curled fingers or pointed toes on that quarter-incher and push or pull perfunctorily.

After three hours, we've disposed of a dozen pitches, feel invincible. We up the ante to 5.10, or extreme difficulty. We slow considerably, but by 2:30 we've climbed 20 pitches: the Half Dome day is history. As a finale, Bachar suggests soloing a 5.11 – an exacting thing for anyone, for this moves us into world-class space. Unless I am abnormally psyched, 5.11 is about my wintertime limit – when I'm fresh and sharp. But now I am exhausted from the past 2,000 feet, having cruised the last four or five pitches on rhythm and momentum. Regardless, we trot over to Intersection Rock, the "hang" for local climbers and the locale for Bachar's final solo.

He wastes no time, and scores of milling climbers freeze when he starts. He moves precisely, plugging his fingertips into shallow pockets on the 105-degree wall. I scrutinize his moves, taking mental notes on the sequence. He pauses at 50 feet, directly beneath the crux bulge. Splaying his left foot onto a slanting rugosity, he pinches a tiny rock wafer and pulls through to a gigantic bucket hold. He walks up the last 100 feet, which is only dead vertical. From the summit, Bachar flashes down a smile, awaiting my reply.

I'm booted up, covered in chalk; I'm facing a notorious climb and the little voice says "No problem." Fifty impatient eyes look me over, as if to say: "Well?" He did make it look simple, I think, stepping on up.

I draw several deep breaths, to convince myself, if nobody else. I do not consider the consequences, only the moves; otherwise, I'd be running in the opposite direction, sane and intact. A body length of easy moves, then those incipient pockets which I finger adroitly before yanking with maximum might. Fifty feet passes quickly. Then, as I splay my left foot up onto the slanting rugosity, the chilling realization comes that, in my haste, I have bungled the sequence, that my hands are too low on that puny wafer that I'm pinching with waning power. My foot is vibrating and I'm desperate, wondering if and when my body will seize and plummet. A montage of black images floods my brain.

I glance beneath my legs and my gut churns at the thought of a free fall onto the boulders. The little voice is bellowing: "Do something! Pronto!" My breathing is frenzied while my arms, gassed from the previous 2,000 feet, feel like iron. Pinching that little wafer, I suck my feet up so as to extend my arm and jam my hand into the bottoming crack above. The crack is too shallow, accepts but a third of my hand. I am stuck, terrified, and my whole existence is focused to a pinpoint.

Shamefully, I understand the only blasphemy – to willfully jeopardize my life, which I have done, and it sickens me. I know that wasted seconds could . . . then the world stops, or is it the preservation instinct booting my brain into hypergear? In a heartbeat I've realized my implacable desire to live, not die! But my regrets cannot alter this situation: arms shot, legs wobbling, head ablaze. My fear overwhelms itself, leaving me hollow and mortified. To concede, to quit, would be easy. The little voice calmly intones: "At least die trying." I agree, and try to punch my hand deeper into the bottoming crack. If only I can execute this one crux move, I'll get an incut jug-hold, can rest off it before the final section. I'm afraid to eyeball my crimped hand, scarcely jammed in the shallow crack. It must hold my 210 pounds on an overhanging wall, and this seems ludicrous, impossible.

My body has jittered in this spot for minutes. My jammed hand says "no way," but the little voice adds "Might as well try it." I pull up slowly – my left foot is still pasted to the sloping edge – and that big bucket hold is right there. I almost have it! I do! Simultaneously my right hand rips from the crack and my left foot flies off the rugosity: all my weight hangs from an enfeebled left arm. Adrenalin powers me to the Thank God bucket where I press my chest to the wall, get that 210 pounds over my feet, and start shaking like no simile can depict.

Ten minutes pass before I consider pushing on. I would rather yank my wisdom teeth with vice grips. Dancing black orbs dot my vision as I finally claw onto the summit. "Looked a little shaky," laughs Bachar.

That night I drove into town and got a bottle. Sunday, while Bachar went for an El Capitan day (3,000 feet), I wandered listlessly through dark desert corridors, scouting for turtles, making garlands from wildflowers, relishing the skyscape – doing all those things a person does on borrowed time.

Under Another Sky

THE OUTBACK! There is no measure, just tones of sun and moon. The red earth curves on the horizon, like open ocean from an open boat. Wildfires crackle through the dun bush, flushing wombats and platypi, setting the spiny anteater afoot. A bloated steer carcass is ravaged by slavering range curs. Everything is a reminder that human life is an intrusion barely tolerated, yet sandstone grottoes depict aboriginal drawings from 20,000 years ago. These vistas of space and light are solitary, and we three feel alone. We're dead lost, smack center in Australia's Northern Territory – the Outback. Lost, in spite of Barry.

Australia's premier outback navigator (by his own appraisal), Barry four days ago had bumped into an old friend, an Aboriginal Elder buying saw blades in Darwin. The Elder mentioned that the aboriginal settlement of Pepimenardi was gearing up for the annual Corrobboree – or ceremony. After a marathon dance the young males would recieve the traditional latticework of chest incisions which, when daubed with salt and excrement, yield the sacred scars. Then circumcision by chipped stone. On the Elder's invitation, we headed out straightaway. D.B. and I went along to escape the stasis of the Darwin pubs, for our plane to New Guinea didn't leave until the next Sunday. Barry, a vibrant, moon-faced lad with an asphalt voice, had veered off the faint dirt road in search of a more direct route, and we had driven in

circles ever since, bouncing and bashing around wafer-like anthills – some 15 feet high – sprouting from the ground in such
numbers they resembled tombstones at a war memorial. Just as
it crossed my mind to chisel our names on one, a shot rang out
– a gunshot. We jeeped off to look for the gunman and found
instead a unique- looking youth booming a soccerball off an
anthill – from forty feet! He looked up, startled.

"Gooday, mates," said the sportsman, "lost, are ya?" A second
shot rang out.

"Not exactly," Barry carped, looking the wise outdoorsman.

"Bullshit!" laughed the sportsman, "nothing out here but cattle
and anthills." The gunman soon arrived, a dead ringer for the
sportsman.

"Gooday; breaking in that new Jeep, are ya?" We laughed, for
bailing wire and crude welding looked to keep the old Jeep erect.

We camped that night with the Moorcroft-Kong brothers,
twenty-one-year-old twins working the summer as range man-
agers, shooting infected cattle and booting their soccerball off
anthills. Half Aboriginal, one quarter English, and one quarter
Chinese, they were reared on a reserve near Ayers Rock, escaping
to a Melbourne secondary school after much recruiting from the
soccer coach. No wonder, since both could run down a dingo,
plus boot a soccerball a country mile. Well-muscled, swarthy,
with tall and angular frames, they had one more year at Univer-
sity before turning pro.

After dinner, the sun hemorrhaged onto sand tinged so red
you'd think it bore the blood of every Aboriginal to suffer the
chipped stone. When we started exchanging lies, Wanbangalang
Moorcroft-Kong mentioned he was Chinese in little more than
name. But, he continued, "I know quite a load about the coolies
who used to work the old gold mines outside Darwin." Barry
and the Kongs instantly raced to the woodpile to pitch huge logs
onto the fire; stretched out under a cobalt sky awash in so many
stars you could not believe it, we started a favorite Australian
pastime – competitive story telling. The game's only rule is that
the story, and every last detail, must ring true. Tradition says a
liar will suffer a quick and grim death. Barry fetched a fifth of
Rare Nugget Scotch, then Wanbangalang began.

"When the colonials first struck big-time gold outside of

Cooktown, they quickly found the task way bigger than their manpower, so they began importing coolies, principally from Hong Kong, although my old man mentioned that a few came from Shanghai and maybe Macao. Anyway, they'd sail south, past the Moslem dynasties in Sumatra and Java, then on down through the Tanimbars. There are Hindus there, real passive people, so they'd usually stop and trade, then sail for Cooktown. Arab ships used to ply this route, looking for Beech-de-mer in the Torres Strait. The coolies came on what was then called the British Cable route. When the Cooktown mines were in full swing, Chinese outnumbered Europeans 7 to 1. Conditions were wretched: coolies were fed on rice and mackeral and paid only one tenth that paid to European miners. The Cooktown mines dried up around 1930, just when they hit at Pine Creek, outside of Darwin; so Hong Kong skippers began to land their passengers at Darwin. Aside from these coolie runs, the British Cable route saw little traffic, just the odd junk bouncing around the Tanimbars, trading porcelain and glass works. My grandfather was captain on one such junk. While sailing from Alor to Wetar, they were brutally ambushed by a Sulu pirate ship. The junk was forced into a remote atoll and scuttled. Many drowned, and many were shot with muskets. The survivors were all diced with sabars, save for six stout males, including my grandfather and great-uncle. They were maimed, then given two casks of water and some sea biscuits before the pirates sailed off for more privateering, intending to snag their new slaves on the return. By coincidence, the six were spotted by a merchant ship packed with coolies heading for Darwin. Emaciated and ravaged by exposure, the six had little choice but to crawl on board and head for life in the mines, though it was some months before their limbs healed.

"In Darwin the coolies stayed devoted to their old ways, eating that putrid food, wearing those silk slippers, the shin-high pants, the lamé vests, the flat hats, the pigtails – everything just as they had back home. They were always together – but not grandpa Kong. After three years, he was fluent in English, had risen to mine foreman, and eventually married Molly Ann Moorcroft, a Welsh maid banished to Australia for embezzlement.

"Notorious for their foreign ways, the coolies did some peculiar things, especially when someone died, and hundreds did. They insisted on shipping the bodies back home, for if a coolie wasn't buried on Buddhist soil, they believed his soul would forever roam the Outback, mingling with abos and wallabies, lost, and there'd never be peace for him. But ships came only three times a year and the voyage took months. My grandfather suggested pickling the stiffs in great oriental urns, with dragons, flames, and all that holy crap painted all over them. It was probably his future wife who suggested saving something beyond the souls, but that's all he had in mind when he interred my great-uncle after a cross-span snapped in an exploratory shaft.

"Anyway, the urns were corked, then stored in a warehouse. To the locals, it became a thing of great intrigue why the coolies would dote so over those urns. The warehouse was never without a crowd of chanting, wailing Chinamen. Many would go there straight from the mines. So much incense smoke lofted from the doors they once thought the place was on fire, and my grandfather had to show the firechief otherwise. Supposedly, that was the only time Europeans ever entered the warehouse, though I suspect Grandmother made quite a few visits – she must have!

"By the time a ship arrived, there were usually dozens of urns for the return trip. In the spring of 1934, when there were stored more urns than usual, a cyclone tore into Darwin and damn near leveled everything. The Chinese morgue was first to go. All those urns spun around the streets, shattering and divesting their grisly cargo. But even as the storm raged, the coolies ranged the streets, ostensibly to salvage the dead and their otehwise doomed souls. Secure in their holds, the locals were dumbstruck to see all those Chinamen brave a cyclone to retrieve some pickled stiffs. It is said, though I hardly believe it, that scores were vacuumed up the twisters's shaft. I do know that Grandfather received broken ribs and wicked contusions for his effort.

"When the storm finally passed, and the authorities started sorting things out, all the urns were reclaimed, save for a few, miraculously intact, found in a bed of rubbish between two surviving buildings. One was slightly cracked, and, when moved, it simply fell apart. And what they found set straight the whole puzzling affair, for in the bottom of the urn lay four inches of gold bullion. Likewise with the others.

"A week later, Grandfather was hanged for grand larceny. My grandmother – Mary Ann Moorcroft – skipped town during the trial, and sixteen years passed before she was picked up in Perth, fencing gilt out of her own steak joint. She had amassed a minor empire, including four restaurants and a string of shrimp boats. Of course, the authorities took it all – even my dad, Sammy Moorcroft-Kong. Then seventeen, he was stuck in a foster home with wayward Aboriginal kids. He fell in love with a full-blooded Aboriginal girl named Ree Wandjina, and they eloped to the reserve in Mukathara. They had six kids, the last two twins, and here we are, mates. And that's fair dinkum!"

Stars shot like hurled sparklers, and the stories flowed with such energy that the Aussies (though hardly us) made impatient listeners. Barry took a shocking chug of Nugget Scotch, shivered, then said, "I suppose you blokes reckon you know the whole story of Ned Kelly, eh?"

The Kongs laughed, talking of Ned's steel suit, his notorious encounters with the law, and the fact that not one Australian was without his own Ned Kelly story. Barry told us his.

"My grandfather, Captain Winston North Bigalow, had just retired from the Royal Marines, where he served under Calhoun at Gallipoli. He settled in the Northern Territory and bought himself a ranch. Life hit hard on the Australian frontier, and certain men were driven to bold, even reckless, designs. One such man was Ned Kelly, a hand on the Captain's ranch. Perhaps he felt trapped as a rancher, or maybe he couldn't endure the tedium of these wide open spaces. Whatever, he took to brooding outside the bunkhouse, talking little, and only then to deride his mates on their complacency. He started dreaming on the job and, despite repeated warnings, grew so listless at the thresher that the Captain sent him packing. But not before Ned stripped choice farm implements of their stainless to forge himself a one-piece cone of body armor, with tiny slits for eyes and two holes for the arms. So garbed, he won infamy as a highwayman, in the mold of a California gunslinger. But the speed of Ned's draw hardly mattered, owing to his indomitable get-up (here Barry held up one hand, like a gun.) Ping! His image soared with each sack. Australia was principally settled by crooks and malcontents, and their offspring found quick identity in Ned Kelly. We had our first Folk Hero. Pass the bottle.

"Now Ned was hardly mobile. His steel suit limited him to the kind of petty jobs which legends are not made of. Still, these capers were greatly exaggerated, and it's probable Ned began trusting his own myth, because he then waged a campaign calling for quick escapes – and he survived only by shooting dead all his foes. Ned started wielding a Gatling gun, descending like a man-o-war. His jobs got bolder and bolder, and while his luck held out, future targets were shoring up should Ned ever strike.

"One sleepy Tuesday morning, when the Captain was making a deposit, Ned Kelly lumbered into that very bank, the terrible churn of his Gatling gun tearing into everything and everybody. By then, Ned's steel suit was riddled with bullet dings from head to shin, and Captain Bigalow, diving behind a great oaken desk, knew the suit was invincible. But as Ned spent his last rounds, the Captain conceived a plan. With the rolling click! of Ned's empty chambers, the Captain sprang from behind the desk. A sharp pop! from his single shot derringer found its mark on Ned's foot – and Ned Kelly fell like a derrick.

"Wounded – Ned got jailed and a heated trial ensued. Thousands lobbied for his acquittal. Sympathizers hadn't felt the hot rip of Ned's bullets and were instead won over by his recklessness. Ultimately, Ned was hanged. But Ned Kelly lives, lives in my son's storybooks, on placemats at the Darwin Inn, on T-shirts strutted on Sydney beaches, and directly above my hearth, where Ned Kelly's steel suit now hangs. I've got a standing bet with anyone who can guess the number of dings on the suit – and I give 1,000-to-1 odds. Pass the bottle."

"I'd wager there's more than a few dings in that story," started Wambangalang, "seeing that I've personallly seen that suit in the National Museum."

"That one's a replica," croaked Barry, "I wouldn't sell the real McCoy for the world."

More trees were pitched on the fire, and we started discussing Aboriginals in general, waiting for some detail to trigger another yarn. We had been to Australia five times now, and D.B. mentioned that the Aboriginals one saw about the towns seemed pretty passive, generally.

"Passive?" questioned Warango Moorcroft-Kong. "No, not passive, just drunk." And he went on to tell us of another side.

"The Aboriginals might now be a defeated race, but their oral tradition admits to times of bravery, courage, and fearsome resistance to enemies. Over the last 200 years, the black fellas have been – at one time or another – everyone's enemy. When we were kids on the reserve, the Elders would entertain us with fantastic tales of creation, when the world was flat and lifeless. Giants arose to venture across the plains, creating mountains, valleys, rivers, and seas. Another favorite was the tale of the golden boomerang, which had such range that it once felled an alien ship whose captured crew were said to have taught the ancient Elders about dreamtime.

"But the oldtimers most enjoyed discussing run-ins with white fellas – heinous accounts of carnage – for it gave vent to the Elders' frustrations and animosities. These stories mostly focused on the halcyon gold rush on the Palmer river, where the Myall Aboriginals killed and ate many diggers. They most relished the Chinamen's flesh, claiming it was less salty, and as savory as the plumpest bandicoot. But the stories always came back to their traditional enemy – the white fellas. Considering the Anglos' penchant for raping Aboriginal women, their systematic plundering of native lands, plus loads of forgotten wrongs . . . well, the white fella could easily find better fellowship. It was not unheard of for a stray prospector to find himself hanging by his thumbs from a gumtree bough. There he'd swing, until every Aboriginal for miles was huddled round, laughing, jeering, and showing with traveling hands just what the white man could look forward to. Kids were sent out to scavenge for the pyre while, with quick swipes, the victim's legs were splintered with clubs. He was then awarded 1,000 cuts with a possum tooth – little, weeping slits from head to toe. The Elders made certain their guest never died before the pyre got stoked. The flame was kept low lest it speed the victim's end. Then they'd carve off a leg, quickly cauterizing the wound with smoldering staffs, prodded close and hard by the rabid mob. Roasted rare over the brief flame, portions were served up to kids, Elders, everyone. They took great pains showing the white fella just how much they savored his flesh. Finally, the victim was forced to eat part of his own leg, an Elder tempting him with the horrid bone. If he refused, faggots were placed on his head, and all gathered round to fan the coals."

Warango shook his head, flipped a pebble into the bonfire, then chuckled, "I doubt any one man got the whole program, but don't doubt for a second that these things did happen. What did they expect? They used to shoot us just for sport . . ."

The heavens glared down like the eyes of a staring crowd, as if the whole universe awaited the next story.

Jungle Crucible

FOR TWO DAYS OUR SITUATION was critical. Then it got desperate. A fever had seized Rick, and his symptoms worsened from dizziness and chills, to vomiting and delirium. Rick was one of six of us attempting the first coast- to-coast traverse of Borneo, a place which time had forgotten, where our native Dyak porters lived as their ancestors did five centuries ago. We were thirty days out – about half way across, we hoped, but hardly knew since even the government topographical maps showed a huge blank in the jungled interior. It was a hellish place to get sick, and the timing couldn't have been worse. We'd been thrashing from one Dyak village to the next, linking them with Dyaks from the former settlement; and some of those villages were no more than a cluster of thatched lean-to's, abandoned when the monsoon raged. The next village – Mahak – was supposedly a large one. We couldn't find it. None of our porters had ever been to Mahak, which we'd battled cruel rain forest to find since leaving the swift Bonai river five days back. A band of nomadic Punan Dyaks said we should have gained Mahak fifteen miles ago. Not bad mileage for an athlete on a track, but to Rick, clawing through the creepers with a raging fever, every step was a mile. We continued through the mud, the thorns, the wasps, and the leeches. The jungle was impenetrable save for the footpath we trudged, and I wondered if we weren't groping around in a big circle. Waning light trickled through the green canopy, but we couldn't see for the smoke.

We broke into a big opening, a slash-and-burn agricultural swath cleaved from a square mile of jungled thicket. The flora had been felled and torched, to be cleared later for rice fields. The hardwoods burn slow, so the fire lasts for months – never a forest fire, but never quite out. The air was hot and hazy and orange-colored in the failing sunlight. Rick, veteran of Everest and K2, was well steeped in adversity, but heat, smoke, and exhaustion had boosted his fever, and he collapsed. I winced at the notion of bivouacing on the spot, which set me pacing. Then I found a note tacked on a banyan tree at trail's edge. The rest of the team had met a Mahak Dyak who assured them the village was only an hour away. Wasted from the previous twenty-five miles, they had pushed on, urging us to follow before nightfall. Dusk was already stealing over the tall trees behind us. The note's last sentence set me cussing: The only trail to Mahak, the one they'd taken, headed straight into the smoke.

For the last four hours, Rick had been able to hike only a hundred yards at a go, yet when I looked at him just then – retching, shaking, wheezing – I knew we had best get on with it somehow or he might never get going again. I put the question to Rick and he instantly gained his feet, ready to plod on. I didn't know how far he could go, and I couldn't consider getting stranded in the oven before us.

The trail was pretty distinct for 100 yards. Then the terrain started rolling, and the trail just disappeared. The only passage followed a string of big trunks spanning white hot logs and reeking coals, far below. The smoke was hateful and the temperature had to be way above 150 degrees. In minutes I couldn't see the perimeter. The setting sun produced a sort of mirage effect that made the way doubly confusing. Worse, we couldn't stop without burning our feet – even through our boots. We followed the nebulous chain of logs which got progressively higher as the temperature rose. Rick looked dead on his feet but continued to wheedle on. He had to: Blue flames leapt from gutted ironwood trunks that flanked us everywhere. My body poured sweat and I struggled with the urge to just run for it.

I freaked when I saw what lay ahead. A hundred-foot smoldering ramin trunk – charred half through – bowed across a channel of waist-deep, red-hot coals. The air rippled from heat rushing off the embers. We couldn't stop and we couldn't turn back, so I cast off before I started analyzing things – just kept looking at the end of that trunk, shimmering in the smoke a long ways off. Half way out the trunk shifted. My hands shot out and sweat popped off the coals below and for a moment I just froze, praying for the trunk to settle in. Breathing little hot breaths, I tiptoed on until, just shy of the cantilevered end, the trunk shifted again. I panicked, galloped a few steps and sprung off the end, just making a smoldering knoll.

I felt like I had led Rick to his death because I knew *he* couldn't pass over that charred trunk. He'd have to try because he had no choice. He was flushed, running sweat, shivering, and I could hear his breathing a hundred feet away. I thought about going back to help him, but even if I could remount the trunk, the walkable surface was only a boot's breadth and charred to shit. Two men's weight might snap it. We traded sorry looks. Rick drew a wheezy breath, then started across. He looked like a drunk on a balance beam, but his feet kept shuffling along. Then the trunk started shifting and his feet were skating all over the black veneer and I couldn't even consider the horror should he pitch into the coals, now twenty-five feet below him. He quavered all the way to the end, then he started getting real woozy and was sucking each breath and looked bone white and finished. Still, he pushed on. He'd extend his front foot out like an antenna, rock onto it, wobble, then repeat the move again. I was gnashing and fretting and yelling "steady man, you've got it" and fully expecting him to plummet off. Miraculously, he gained the very end and I screamed "jump man, you've got to jump"; but it wasn't in him. He grimaced hard, then half fell, half hopped towards me. I got an arm, pulled, and we tumbled back, rolling up with wicked blisters about our arms and legs. Rick draped both arms over my shoulders and I plowed through shallow embers towards the perimeter, only one-hundred feet beyond. We finally escaped the slash-and-burn inferno, and collapsed once we regained the trail.

Rick was jaded to the brink of human endurance, and *still* wished to push on, to get it over. His fever had first struck while dragging dugouts up white water, three days back. Then two twelve-hour jungle tromps. And now it's dark and he wants to push on and I coudn't figure what kept this guy going. Probably Mahak, which we thought had to be close.

It was not.

We trudged another half-hour through tall stalks of sugarcane that hedged the dark trail, now lit by a rising moon and swarms of fireflies. We'd been going for over fifteen hours. We stopped. Rick breathed in hideous, reedy gasps, almost hyperventilating. Whatever had him, had him good.

Off again. We turned a corner and there it was: A six-hundred-foot longhouse with dozens of natives huddled around our teammates on the veranda. Straightaway we were ushered into the Chief's rooms. Clad in briefs and with jowls bulging of betel nut, he rolled out a rattan mat and Rick collapsed. We had to get him rehydrated, but nothing stayed down, and we were helpless to do anything but watch him writhe on the mat, more dead than alive. His hours were numbered, so we were astounded when the chief told us that Mahak had a seldom-used grass air strip and that a missionary pilot was scheduled to visit the next day! The chief warned that, though the missionary pilot's word was gold, his puny, single engined Cessna was often checked by coastal squalls.

But fate finally swung Rick's way when the plane's echo volleyed through the haze the next morning. Now a withered wraith, Rick was accorded priority over sacks of rice and sugar, and the missionary volunteered his home until locating help. He said there were no proper hospitals even on the coast, but the oil companies maintained clinics which, he believed, would accept outsiders in a pinch. We bid Rick goodbye, and while he arced into the clouds, *we* were left hanging. What could he have that could thrash him so bad, so fast? Were we next? We would wonder for the next twenty days.

•

Our backs were tweaked from the eighteen-mile hump around suicidal rapids on the lower Kayan. Equatorial sun had fried us alive as we charged down steaming waters below the portage. We were weak and emaciated. Tanjun Sellor – the first civilized settlement in months – looked like El Dorado. It was right there, two-hundred yards off, and while the bamboo dock started teeming with curious folk, amongst the chocolate natives we couldn't mistake Rick's face, shriveled and sallow, but very much alive. As our little neoprene raft banged into the pylons, we reached out to make sure he was real. He recounted his ghastly hallucinations, his toes curling and skin wrinkling from dehydration, his massive I.V.'s in his life-and-death struggle with typhoid, possibly complicated with malaria. The clinic was staffed with civilians, with the German doctor only making cameo visits. By fluke, the doctor had arrived concurrently with Rick. He also had Ringer's lactate (I.V.'s) and Fanzadar (for malaria), both mighty rare in these parts. By all estimates, another day in Mahak would have been Rick's last. The chance he should fall ill just shy of Mahak was one in thirty, while the odds that a plane should land the next day were twice that – to say nothing of surviving the slash-and-burn epic which I barely made in perfect health.

The next day we gained the east coast of Kalimantan and dined with the missionaries that had seen Rick through. While we marveled at the clockwork of chance that had delivered Rick intact, the missionaries wrote the whole thing off to divine intervention, which sounded marvelous. I expected an apt verse of Job, but it never came. It should have, for when looking back on Rick's miraculous luck, even us heathens had to say – Ah-men!

Adios, Cueva Humboldt

SINCE ENTERING THE HUGE cave, two miles back, we had followed a flat and easy tourist path, uneventful but for the squawking guachero birds who couldn't see much, and who constantly careened off huge stalagmites. Then, through some geological wonder, the whole cave pinched down to a keyhole, which we crawled through in utter silence save for the slosh of ankle-deep water. Just ahead, the ceiling dropped down to a little, inverted V-slot known as the Channel – the water had risen to eye level.

"Ay, mis juevos!" gasped Delgado, a local expert we had enlisted to lead us to the climbing. Apparently, one should cram his head into the V-slot, then tread fifty feet to open passage. We trained our lights down the little channel but couldn't see much. A rapid pant, and in went Delgado, thrashing and churning for minutes. Then: "No hay problema, gringos !" A surge of claustrophobia washed over me, and I felt like turning back. But I could hardly do this after conning D.B.to come all the way to Venezuela for this very cave.

•

The Cueva Humboldt (or Cueva Guachero) is the most celebrated cavern in South America. The name comes from the itinerant German naturalist, Alexander von Humboldt, said to have done the initial exploration in 1799. Considering that the Caripito Indians have lived there since the moon rose, it seems likely that they did the first snooping, not the Baron. He did, however, conduct a comprehensive study of the guacheros – a very rare bird, indeed – as well as some sketchy ethnology on the local Indians. Two hundred years ago, Humboldt noted, the horrible warbling of the guacheros (guachero: one who cries and laments) discouraged most superstitious Indians from exploring the cave. Maybe the Baron *was* first. Considering the obscure location, it's amazing that a German naturalist made his way to Caripe in 1799. Whatever, a bigger-than-life statue of Humboldt stands nearby, with chiseled jaw and aquiline nose.

Rich oral and written traditions surround the Cueva Humboldt. The oral is utterly fantastic, combining myths, superstitions, and half truths. As claimed by a promotional brochure, the written history is "uniform," which means that all the writers have agreed upon the same fables. Accordingly, in the early 1900s, a second German group survived the first keyhole crawl, but were held up at a curtain of stalactites; returning, they punched through with a sledgehammer. The cool waters rose with each step, and oral tradition says the Germans withdrew when their privates froze, just short of the Channel. In a photodocumented case, an Italian team slipped through the Channel to venture another ten miles, encountering a baffling maze of passages and fabulous chambers. These were all given Italian names, which were changed to Spanish when, in 1964, a team from Sociedad Espeleologicolia de Caracas explored, surveyed, mapped, and spray-painted to cave's end, 15 miles into the mountain. Aside from the Channel, and a few rock steps, it's a safe and sane journey trekking to the Virgin Room, where progress is checked by smooth, featureless limestone, and where a small brass idol of Mary cradles Jesus in a blanket. For each of the four or five (average) annual expeditions, it has become the custom to buff up Jesus' face, giving it a penetrating sheen under a headlamp. Recent parties have produced a cartographical map, which park superintendent Leopoldo de la Rubia had shown me on my first visit.

An ardent caver, Leopoldo fetched a stack of maps, then a photo of a gigantic golina – actually, a huge plug missing from the mountain, like a uniform crater. "Golina" comes from a similar Slavic word for circular valley, according to Leopoldo. He pushed several maps together on the cement floor, gushed a flood of Spanish too swift for me to understand, pointed to various incomprehensible numbers on the overlapping charts, and concluded that the golina lay directly above the Italian Room, half a mile short of the cave's end. With a flurry of arms, Leopoldo described the Italian Room, which is roofed by a great maw – so big, in fact, that no light can reach the zenith. Then Leopoldo drew close, too close, for his breath reeked of garlic and cheroots. His eyes peeled, and he spoke in hushed tones, like he was divulging King Tut's other tomb. Leopoldo reckoned that a crafty climber could easily link the cave with the golina. It would be like scaling the interior of an open hourglass, and this is something that cavers and fools dream about. But why would Leopoldo tell me this, unless he too expected to go? He did. Unfortunately for Leopoldo, when I finally returned, nine months later, Leopoldo was at a symposium in Barcelona. There was little else for us to do but thrash through that freezing Channel on our own.

•

It was no big thing, that Channel, if you didn't mind raking your head and face across the limestone. You stayed where the air was, and it was tight. We had to make four laps apiece to drag all our gear through, one pack at a time. On the last haul, our 600-foot rope snagged at mid-channel, so we took turns going underwater to feel for the hitch, later to lurch up and receive hateful knots about the head. We almost left it.

After stooping and crabbing beneath a low ceiling – for a mile – we gained the first rock step, where a greasy rope hung over a thirty-foot vertical tongue of flowstone. Delgado handwalked up without a word. D.B. followed, barely making it with his hundred-pound load, variously scattered between soaking ropes, racks of muddy pitons, and two unwieldy packs. "Shit!" he exclaimed.

"What's up?" I asked, untying the rope.

"Oh, the anchor's just a little slim."

"Hey, eets limestone, hombres," started Delgado, "fuerte. . ."

I huffed up to find the cord clove-hitched off to a thumb- sized stone mushroom.

"Fuerte!" stressed Delgado. D.B. scoffed, booted the limestone thumb. It popped clean and the rope snaked down into black.

Delgado looked confused. I wrestled the 600-foot rope onto my shoulder and we booked.

Considering the cave's vastness and the countless aberrations, the going was pretty straightforward, mostly scrambling, a little groveling over and around hazards, with limited crawling through thick mud, a murderous job with our loads.

Punctuating the connecting arteries, colossal chambers bore square, milky boulders and telephone-pole stalagmites. Great diaphanous crystals studded the walls, twinkling like rhinestones. Only a troop of spotlights could reveal the cave's secrets. Struggling with loads in one hundred percent humidity, we just pushed on.

By any definition, we didn't know a damn thing about caving. I had puttered around a couple jive caves in California, and D.B. and I had nearly gotten ourselves killed in a New Guinea cavern. Otherwise, we had no experience at all, and after about five hours of slogging, I started getting a case of nerves. It's just the misery of these huge loads, I thought.

When we finally arrived at the Italian Room, seven hours in, we were mud-covered and lackadaisical. A glance at the labyrinthian ceiling showed us that our plan looked anything but the small affair that Leopoldo de la Rubia had avowed. We had figured as much, lugging big loads of climbing gear.

"This thing looks horrendous," D.B. moaned. But once the steam stopped billowing off our bodies and the humidity became bearable, the knowledge that we didn't have to lug those damn packs anymore quickly elevated our spirits. Seated in the mud, we lit up cigars and started scanning the huge roof with our flashlights. D.B. said he felt like Tycho Brahe, the ancient astronomer who had worked exclusively with the naked eyeball – and who was almost always wrong.

We had hoped for a uniform chimney leading straight to daylight. A silly notion. Halfway through my cigar, I felt my neck all kinked up. We had not a clue where to begin. The ceiling appeared as a confusion of twisting tunnels, spiraling aretes, gaping shafts – like a dome of wormwood.

"This thing looks totally horrendous," D.B. moaned.

Finally, we chose a vertical ramp-and-gully system that seemed to gain the upper wall most straightforwardly. Without a huge lighting system, any choice was a shot in the dark. As I rooted through the climbing gear, Delgado wished us luck, then left, promising to return in two days. Delgado hadn't said ten words the whole day, so we had little to judge him on.

"Think we can find our way out of here?" I asked D.B.

"Don't know," D.B. answered. We did not expect to see Delgado again.

D.B. climbed up to what we had hoped was a good ledge below the first ramp, but he informed me it was a "big-ass sump." Hand traversing around the sump would require some protection lest D.B. get shishkabobed on the stalagmites below. D.B. slapped in some dull pitons, clipped the rope through, then traversed to the ramp on sloping holds. Gazing up at the bulging ramp, we realized the problems. The lead rope, soaked from the Channel, weighed thirty pounds easy; the 600-foot trail rope handled like a trans-Atlantic phone cable. We were mud-covered, steamed as a smudgepot, and starting up a soapy limestone ramp with only a feeble headlamp as a guide . . . .

"Watch me close!"

Scraping the mud off his shoes, D.B. headed up, splaying his legs on the offset walls, blasting pitons, and grunting horribly. After eighty feet, D.B., now just a faint glow, said he couldn't advance without tunes. I fumbled through the pack, nabbed the blaster, and punched in Wilfredo Vargas. Owing to the cave's fantastic acoustics, my two-bit Indonesian tape deck roared.

Snug in an alcove, D.B. yelled down for me to jumar up. The pitons came out all too easily.

We walked 30 feet from the alcove to where the gully resumed. Soon the gully changed from a rubbly slot to a bulging, geological wonder, with huge ivory horns, horizontal purple spears, teetering smoked crystals, and countless stone roots twisted in bizarre, electrified patterns. My pitons were very poor, but tying off an organ-pipe crystal wouldn't help – too fragile. The holds were loose or detached, and when treading them grew too nervy, I had to burrow deep into the vertical gully. Just above me, a huge chockstone blocked passage. A mystery held it in place, and a whisper would look to dislodge it. I hadn't set a decent piton in 100 feet, and mounting the chockstone seemed mad: it was just too big and too loose. Rather, I started shimmying up behind it, holding my breath. Eventually lodged, I stretched up for a big hold, then started yarding my hips through the wee space between the chockstone and the gully. The chockstone pivoted, then popped! It roared down the gully like mortar fire. I screamed. As D.B. dove for the alcove, the glittering chockstone exploded into a billion ingots precisely where he had stood.

"Nice shot !" D.B. deadpanned.

Just ahead, the gully eased and a shale ramp led toward a big, flat notch forty feet above. Every move sent down massive shale, so I finally told D.B. to hide in the alcove. I plowed up to the notch, the loose crap whizzing downward. A discontinuous crack system rifled up a vertical face above. The rock proved too brittle to take bolts, simply exploding when drilled. It would take pitons, however, so I walloped home half a dozen and brought D.B. up. He arrived in full smoke, and we carefully checked the rope for chops. It seemed impossible that the lead rope wouldn't have been damaged by either the chockstone or the shale, but that seemed to be the case.

Preparing for the next lead, we didn't talk much lest we start analyzing what lay overhead. You can spend a lifetime adventuring, yet still count on one hand the times when things get so outrageous that nothing could have prepared you for them. When this happens, you know immediately, because the experience is so intimidating that you carry on in a state of half shock. That shock, that boundless exhilaration, is the earmark of the true whopper; and I was never so sure of this when, ankle deep in shale, I gazed at the black void overhead.

D.B. set off, thunking his miserable pitons. I lounged on the shale, listening to music. D.B. reached a ledge after three hours, and I jumared up. Had this been granite, the pitch would have been moderate; but this brittle soap afforded little for the pegs, which came out with a single hammer blow. Good thing he didn't rip. From D.B.'s shelf, I tiptoed left to start free climbing up a loose flake. After 30 feet, sans protection, the wobbles came on strong and I just managed a piton before my muddy boots blew off the holds. From there I encountered continuously grim artificial climbing, gingerly clipping my three-step stirrups into a creaking string of pitons. I ran out of gear after 100 feet, whaled in the last pitons – which were wretched – then set up an anchor hanging from slings. As D.B. came up, I started quaking.

Dangling in the black, dreaming up all kinds of ridiculous horrors, I dialed up the tape deck and pretended I was hanging from a coat rack in a closet. Waiting for his body to stop steaming, D.B. re-racked the gear, then led off. By the sound of the pitons and his constant quibbling, the rock degenerated even worse. Two hours and three tapes went by, as the thunk-thunk of pitiful pitons bandied about.

"Hey, there's a cave up here!"

"A what?"

"A cave!"

"We're *in* a cave, you blockhead."

"Okay, a hole in the wall, a tunnel, a cleft, a subway, whatever. How much rope left?"

"Twenty feet."

"I'll just make it."

Drenched in salsa music, I stoked a fresh cigar, smiling at the notion of escaping these hanging stances, if only momentarily. After another few songs, I got word to ascend the rope "very smooth-like," since the only anchor was "a sling looped around a schist gargoyle."

"A what?!" No reply. I tested the rope, which seemed to be tied off, and started up. Some of the pitons had already fallen out, and the bulk of the others didn't require a hammer to remove.

We hoped to find the bottom of the golina soon, or some escape. We'd better. My conservative estimate had us about 650 feet off the cave floor. The rock had become flaky trash, and the prospect of more artificial climbing set me quaking. Fifty feet shy of the curious anchor, I started yelling for details, got none, and arrived at the subway with D.B. absent. That bit about a schist gargoyle proved a gag; the rope was secured to a spider's web of chockstones. Steaming, I dumped the gear and made my way down the flat subway, banking that it led to the golina. D.B. appeared just as the subway opened and turned snow white. From nervous release, or pure astonishment, we both started laughing. Nothing could hope to duplicate this unique passage, decked in thick, alabaster crystal.

We crawled, shimmied, and walked another thirty minutes. A

porthole-sized slot veered off our ivory shaft, but we kept on, hoping for something straightforward. Soon the subway angled down abruptly into what our headlamps claimed was another big chamber. Of course we'd need a rope to descend, which entailed an hour's round trip back to the gear. Once there, I peered over the lip of the subway, gazing straight down into the void we had just wrestled with. We were in no hurry to resume that hideous, blind, aid climbing, so we hustled back to the new chamber, set a funk anchor, then rappelled – not into another gorgeous room, but straight into a mud pit the size of my small apartment, and similarly appointed. The walls were featureless, the air dank and heavy. Then D.B. spotted a little tunnel at the mud line. Our headlamps showed it to open up in twenty feet – to a bottomless hole or another crystalline ballroom, we couldn't tell. I crawled in feet first, boring the chest-tight slot with my feet churning like a back-hoe. We traded off, booting quite a load into that chamber.

Once we could snake in two body lengths, we started talking about a rope; but that rope presently hung over the rappel and wouldn't quite stretch to the crawl. D.B. wallowed back in. A muffled sound, silence, then a distant splat! Wild cussing fired from the hole. I quickly snaked in head first, an inconceivable concept a minute back. The floor had collapsed just short of the new room, plunging D.B. into a quagmire twenty feet below. Closet sized, the new room led nowhere. D.B., knee deep in primordial ooze, didn't look altogether pleased. He raked his hands through the soup, vainly searching for his headlamp. The mud forbade climbing out, and I didn't have anything long enough for a handline. We talked about options, though we knew there were none.

So I left D.B., left him in shocking darkness, knee-deep in a sewer, twenty feet down a mud closet, a mile into a virgin shaft, 650 feet up a limestone wall, over ten miles inside a cave, in Caripe, Venezuela, South America. Aside from Davy Jones' place, there ain't no lonelier locker.

When, just past the white room, my light started flickering, I freaked. Considering my breakneck pace, my guess had the gear only five, possibly ten minutes away. More sprinting. When my headlamp tapered to a candle, I raged. To think they called this a special battery, good for 24 hours. Sitting back, I checked my watch to find we'd been going strong for almost 30 hours. Then: darkness.

A wave of terror snapped me upright. My head banged off the low ceiling; I cursed and sat back down. Luckily, the way ahead was walkable, uniform, and without detours. My cigarette lighter was more psychological relief than anything, since I could only keep it going for 20 seconds before it felt like a meteor. The journey to the gear – probably 200 feet – took almost three hours of fumbling, bashing, falling, and raging; I discovered every ankle-wrenching slot. When the lighter finally melted, I was only 50 feet from the gear, but I took to crawling to avoid a free- fall exit from the subway. At last, I stumbled over the packs to play blind man's bluff rooting for the spare lights. Finally, with a click – reborn! We had four extra headlamps and loads of batteries. Grabbing these and a spare rope, I bolted directly for D.B., pressing for greater speed, paying the price in contusions.

Once down in the mud room, I quickly tied the new rope off, clipped on a pair of ascenders, stuck a bight of rope in my teeth, and burrowed back into the pit. D.B., sunk to mid-chest, was so unresponsive that ten minutes passed before he came around, squinting, mumbling, and looking sorely worked. Shortly after my departure he had grown so distressed that he rabidly churned the mud for his headlamp, all the while sinking deeper into the mire. When movement was almost impossible, and submersion imminent, he plunged into a ghastly swoon complete with hallucinations. I crawled back into the mud room. Soon the line came taut, and when D.B. re-emerged, it all came back to him. "Holy Mother of God!" Wild eyed, bearing six inches of mud, he looked like something from a Japanese thriller. We could only collapse into the mud, howling.

The hump back to the gear passed in a stupor. When we passed the one and only aberration, the little porthole crawlway, D.B. joked that we should immediately explore it. I didn't break stride. Back at the gear we swilled a gallon of water and started rifling for food; but we both slumped back unconscious before the first can got opened.

D.B. scratched around in black distress, searching for spare batteries. We had fallen asleep with our lights on, and they had since gone dead. D.B. carried on, cussing, while my mind came back to now. "We didn't leave the pack in that mud room, did we?"

Oh, shit. "We couldn't have," I countered, the mere notion popping me into fresh consciousness. D.B. had the light and batteries in his hands and didn't produce light until I had started a panicked search and was screaming, near tears. "Click! Just kidding." "You bastard!." For another ten minutes my body surged with adrenalin at the prospect of blindly thrashing back to the mud room.

I was set to quit this cavern, but after wolfing down our entire foodstuffs, we psyched for a last jaunt back into the subway – to inspect that porthole passage. We had three headlamps apiece, plus pockets bulging with batteries. I would curl up and die before again facing that horrible darkness, a sensation that no prose can even approximate. We powered past the white room, gaining the porthole crawl soon enough. I headed in. Once through the stricture, the shaft merged into a massive, multi-layered catacomb of meandering tubes. A quick retreat for a guideline. We spent the next hours groveling through the vast arteries, pursuing independent lines. After a solid dose of belly crawling, my knees and elbows were raw, my nerves shot. One could spend years groping through, in, up, and around this cave, never finding that damn golina. On the crawl back to the subway, my headlamp flickered, and I screamed. Later my chest got stuck and I nearly wept. "Let me out of here!" We lumbered back to the gear, resigned to resume climbing.

The wall above the subway overhung gently, but a flared crack reluctantly accepted gear deep in its cleavage. I gazed straight down into the 650-foot void, shivered, then started up. After 40 feet, the crack melted into a rounded groove, with no crack and no chance to place any kind of gear. The rock degenerated into loose mortar, and, as before, it simply flaked away when drilled. Free climbing was impossible. I pendulumed around, looking for options. Then the top piton popped, hurling me down an unexpected 20 feet. "That's it!"

"We're licked," groaned D.B. "Let's get the hell out of here!" I lowered back into the subway. In one minute, we didn't care that we had come all the way to Venezuela and still failed. It was get out or go mad.

We started the long descent, a six-hour epic, tedious and dreadful. On the long trudge out of the main chamber, we ran into Delgado. He had tales of his own epic, for when D.B. had booted off that puny stone mushroom/anchor at the first rock step, the rope had tumbled down with it, leaving a treacherous descent for poor Delgado. Furthermore, he had to re-climb it, bare-handed, to presently get here, a feat he claimed was equal to anything we had done. We couldn't disagree.

Four hours passed before we reached that rock step, knowing only two miles remained to open air. I was not excited about trusting a rope hitched off to some tenuous wart, so I searched for something more substantial. D.B. doubled a rope around a stout pillar and we three descended.

Now we trucked in earnest, knowing only the 50-foot Channel lay between us and a trot to freedom. But the cave would serve up a final garland. Trying to simultaneously haul two packs through the Channel, Delgado went and got his foot stuck. After about an hour of wiggling and yanking, I was not only hypothermic, but ferociously vexed. It just didn't seem that Delgado's foot was all that stuck. He could wiggle it around but it still wouldn't come loose. An absurd idea occurred to me, and Delgado admitted as much: he wouldn't pull so hard as to lose his shoe. When D.B., now livid, told him he had 30 seconds before we left, his foot slid free like a knife from butter. But poor Delgado was crestfallen. I had little choice but to swim back in and find his damn shoe. After another 15 minutes, D.B. said he would buy him ten new shoes. No good. I finally found it floating ten feet past the Channel.

We all shivered convulsively when finally making the tourist path, breaking into a jog, hoping to warm up and possibly exit before dark. Soon the cave's ragged lip arched in faint relief against the darkening sky. Thousands upon thousands of guacheros swarmed into the twilight, where clouds and stars and moon and all kinds of open space kept my feet shuffling until I nearly tackled Humboldt's statue. For no reason whatsoever, I surveyed the Baron's face, actually touching his chiseled jaw. D.B. bounded about, screaming at the new moon. We had been inside for about 65 hours, had slept six. I backpedaled, dropped to my knees, and kissed the ground: Adios, Cueva Humboldt.

Improbable Marksman

SINCE IT HAD NOT RAINED in 13 days, which seemed impossible, the river had waned to a purl, and we could hike its normally flooded banks – skating over slick riverstones submerged for a thousand years, stones which would never feel direct sunlight until the invincible green ceiling had receded; and by then, the stones would be sand, or silt, whisked into larger rivers, washed into deltas, into the ocean.

We were five people: a native Iban chief, whose torso was a study in primal tatooing, and whose bare feet crunched over driftwood littering the pebbly bank; two Iban youths, who carried our foodstuffs in swollen rattan packs, and whose constant mouthfuls of betel nut yielded a vile spit which stained the light river stones bright red; a young Malaysian soldier assigned to us for reasons only a third world nation could conceive of, whose World War II issue Browning was held aslant his chest, poised to fire; and me, who was not going to drag a film crew unto darkest Sarawak until I had seen the elusive lost tribe, felt thin, bark skin clothes, tasted stout borak. But I had all but forgotten about the lost tribe because over the previous two days I'd become intrigued, confused, then consumed by one question: why did the soldier shadow the chief with his ready gun, safety off, fingers twitching, looking to blow the chief's head off if he should so much as sneeze?

At first I thought little of it – just daft Malaysian police. I'd spent enough time in Asia to know about authorities and their guns. They'll wield them, flourish them, direct traffic with them, just because they have one and you don't. But here? We were miles into forgotten jungle and the soldier would stumble because he wouldn't for a second take his eyes off the chief, an unarmed man easily 25 years his senior.

Even more confusing was how the soldier so revered the chief, fetching fronds for the chief's bed, giving him the first, and biggest servings of rice. Conversely, the chief fathered the soldier, chuckling at his lack of junglecraft, showing him just how to swing a machete. Their minds addled by the nut, the young Ibans spat their mouthfuls, unconcerned that their master was tracked point blank. But still more baffling was what happened at night.

Our first bivouac involved chopping out the vines between the flukes of a soaring banyan and sleeping in a partitioned circle, heads to the trunk. The soldier had strung his gun from a dangling liana, ten feet away. The insects, unchallenged by rain or wind, were deafening. Still, I could hear the chief and the soldier's conversation, and occasional laughs, for an hour after we retired. I couldn't understand much, and guessed the content by the tone. Finally, it was just the insects and me; but I couldn't take my eyes off the dark profile of the rifle, spinning slowly.

The soldier was not hazing me, so I couldn't reckon why I should care about any of this. I'm not sure I did care. My intrigue came from the utter weirdness of it all. I took to my feet to see if everyone was actually sleeping. Not a move. Finally I realized that the gun was empty, the shells secure in this soldier's pocket. Of course. I pulled the sheet over my head and slipped into a doze.

We were not driven from our berth by rain, as expected. But for the solid green canopy we couldn't get a peep at the sky. I watched the soldier untie his rifle from the liana, waiting for him to thumb a shell into the chamber. I so expected this that we had slogged half a mile before I acknowledged that he had not. I was absolutely sure that he had not.

The soldier resumed his ludicrous vigil; the chief, in the lead, moved along the intricate riverbank, the soldier always an arm's length behind, stumbling over roots, into potholes, his glare never leaving the chief – and as always, his rifle poised, ready to fire. That he should continue this, with an empty gun, reduced him from a brute to a rare type of fool, a child lost in a deranged game of charades. I still found this facinating, but gave it no more thought. The leeches were starting to get bad, anyway.

The weather held. I noticed everyone (but the soldier) stealing looks at the surrounding jungle, towering in twisted madness and ancient shade. Everyone dreaded the monsoon's return, when in minutes, the river could flood, forcing us into spiked, squelchy ripe thicket which angled up sharply from the comparatively easy passage of the riverbank.

In late afternoon, we stopped for the night on a huge sand bar which curved with the river's sharp bight. It took the young Ibans and me thirty minutes to clear the flotsam – girthy trunks and limbs washed there during ultra-high water. Meanwhile, the chief and the soldier, talking and clowning, collected dry twigs for a fire in the lee of a mammoth ramin trunk which we couldn't even budge.

The young Ibans and I tumbled down the sand bar and spent an hour damming the river. But no fish ever came. When we clawed back up onto the sand bar, I noticed the gun laying on the ramin trunk. For an unknown reason, for no reason, I went over to the rifle, feigned to shoulder it, sighting a distant target, then: Bang! I shouted out. The little line of hairs danced on the soldier's lip. He grabbed the rifle, flipped off the safety, shouldered it, aiming at the river, then: Bang! The report so surprised me that I fell back onto the sand. The Ibans belly laughed. I watched astonished as the soldier ejected a smoldering shell onto the sand, replaced it, flipped on the safety, then casually laid the rifle back onto the trunk, a tendril of blue smoke lofting off the band. The soldier returned to the fire, and on the chief's cue, apportioned us all servings of rice – big dollops of steaming gunk, the first and biggest slid to the chief on a banana leaf.

Now the chief and the soldier talk like father and son. They must have some tacit understanding, some kind of truce for these leisurely hours. I cradled my mountain of rice and took a seat on the trunk, one foot from the rifle: no one even looked up from his banana leaf.

Why anyone should appear ready to shoot someone dead, but at the same time, have no intention of shooting anyone at all, seemed unfathomable. I'd let the future sort things out; but the riddle wouldn't let me alone, and my mind kept turning it over.

That night, the soldier's snoring kept me up, though I could hardly hear it above the bugs. Still, I felt like grabbing the gun and blowing his brains out, which would at least solve my anxiety. I had not thought about the lost tribe for two days.

It still hadn't rained, so we broke camp shortly after sun up, anxious to put some dry miles behind us. We had two options: a round-about jungle thrash, or a direct route following the riverbed through a steep valley. The chief chose the riverbed. We'd have to move fast, for the trek through the ravine would take six hours or more, and should it start raining suddenly, and violently, we'd get flooded out if we were not well along. As I made out in my poor Malay, there was little escaping the ravine into the jungle – just too steep. The chief held his hand up vertically, and nodded for effect.

We entered the ravine after about an hour. Though the canyon walls rose directly from the river, the streambed was wide – easily 300 feet across – so I figured us safe since the water was spread out slow and shallow. I felt it would take a deluge ten hours to fill the canyon, or for the river to rise high enough to add to the scores of splintered logs teetering atop twenty foot river boulders.

Shortly, the walls reared up vertically on both sides, spangled with dripping red orchids, where thick, corkscrew vines spiraled down from the heights – dark and errant guy wires – looping and crossing in the river, then sweeping back up the opposite bank. We stopped.

The chief gave a short speech, his outstretched arm waving to one, then the other canyon wall. He emphasized words which I did not understand. The soldier nodded quickly, many times, sweat pouring off his face; but his mien said he wouldn't be cowed by the chief's bombast, that he'd persist with his mission. He twice checked the safety, making sure it was off. The chief nodded, turned, and resumed the march, his black eyes traveling between the canyon walls: the soldier's eyes were burning holes through the chief's back.

The chief barked an angry phrase which drew the soldier so close I doubt there was a rifle's length between them. I followed the soldier nearly as closely as he shadowed the chief, trading glances between the two, quite enjoying the mad drama. On both sides, the young Ibans flanked out.

The chief stopped suddenly, silently raising one hand: the young Ibans froze; but the soldier jumped and for the first time, he moved the rifle away from his chest. His knees flexed, and I thought: Now he's going to gun him down – for stopping, for raising his hand. The soldier's face had a nervous, expectant look all over it. Finally, the chief dropped his gaze away from the cliffside, lowered his hand, and marched on. The soldier fell into file.

It was deathly hot. I almost choked on the humidity. I marched alongside, staring at the soldier, never knowing exactly where he looked, since his pupils were so dark I couldn't get a fix on them. I just sloshed on, drunk with adrenalin, expecting to see a man shot in the back. I imagined the chief, face down in the river. I imagined worse things, and I admit my fascination with it all.

When on both sides the canyon wall shot up hundreds of feet, the chief quit scanning the cliffs and we started hiking very fast. In another hour, the angles eased, and holes started appearing in the thick canopy through which gleamed shafts of blistering sunlight.

We slowed, the chief again scoping the cliffsides, at what, I couldn't possibly guess since it all looked like the same green brawl. The chief hiked a route which avoided any sloshing, any direct sunlight – a quiet, stealthy route. When the soldier stumbled, the chief shot him a glance which I thought would cost the chief; but the soldier only nodded. I noticed the soldier's gun shook horribly, and I didn't care. My confusion had turned into impatience for something to happen. I smelled blood, and a copper taste hung on my tongue.

Then it all happened so fast.

The chief treaded lightly along a spit of gravel, three creeping shadows playing across the dark, still water to our left. For several minutes the chief's eyes had been fixed about 200 feet up the righthand wall. With a last step so slow it took some balance to perform, the chief's hand came up; and with his eyes still riveted up and right, he froze. The soldier froze. Flanked out on both sides, the young Ibans froze. I froze; and during the long second that followed, my heartbeat drowned out the shrieking insects.

Suddenly, the chief wheeled around. The soldier extended the gun at arm's length, one hand clasping the middle of the barrel, the other, the very butt of the stock. In one fluid motion, the chief snatched the rifle, shouldered it and turned, could hardly have aimed, then: Boom! A crisp flame leaped from the muzzle as the report banged off the canyon walls, bandied up and out the holes in the canopy. I perceived a faint dark object rolling down the right wall, tumbling with greater and greater speed. I finally locked onto it as it plunged over a last, vegetated ceiling and splashed into a deep pool 100 feet away.

No sooner had it broke the water when the young Ibans were onto it, machetes drawn. But it hardly mattered. The chief was a dead- eye: a gaping hole right through the deer's head – a brain shot.

I spun to face the chief, but he had already wandered off downstream, his eyes fixed high on the left wall. Fumbling with excitement, the young soldier struggled to thumb another bullet into the chamber, fumbled mainly because he kept looking up to see how far the chief had advanced. Gun loaded, safety off, the soldier scampered off to take up his position, walking quietly, and in step behind the chief.

Down and Out

"Dear Mr. Long,

. . . Lastly, pursuant to Article Seventeen in National Park Regulations, the device of air to ground transfers is strictly prohibited. Likewise, even traditional parachuting is limited to emergencies. Consequently, we cannot accord you exception without setting an illegal precedent. Thank you for considering Parks National as a proposal site for your filming, and good luck in finding another location . . . ." and so it ran, from the superintendent of the Canadian National Parks. In other words, no cliff jumping on Baffin Island. I had foolishly presumed the legality by dint of Rick Sylvester's James Bond jump, unaware that directly following it, Article Seventeen had been drafted to prohibit another. I'd spent thousands of company funds in preproduction, and the show had been sold on the strength of what I'd sworn would provide outlandish footage. Now the show's centerpiece had backfired, leaving me only ten days to find another site – no mean task when the jump had to break the current world's record of 4,600 feet. And where to find another 5,000-foot overhanging cliff? Nepal? India? Both the company and the network were staring me down.

Sweating bullets, I made for the home of Carl and Jean Boenish, the husband and wife team who had organized, popularized, and labored to legitimize the mad practice of leaping off fixed objects. They had founded a group entitled BASE, an acronym denoting 1) Buildings, 2) Antennae, 3) Spans (bridges), 4) Earth; these the various props off which they plunge. Carl had championed the first wave of El Capitan jumps and had since traveled the world, filming, jumping, writing, and preaching the virtues of BASE jumping. His wife, Jean, was equally avid, with over forty BASE jumps to her credit. As I would learn, Jean had the more athletic skills, plus an invincible composure that baffled me throughout. Should anyone know of an alternative site, Carl and Jean would. I threw my car into overdrive and powered to their Hawthorne home, ready to deal.

Carl, a craggy-faced, bouncy 43-year-old of contagious enthusiasm, had once visited my office. He was all business then, and a steely dealer he was, inflexible in fee and procedure. Now, after explaining my predicament, he relaxed, for I lay over a barrel. Consequently, quite a different fellow emerged. Jean, nineteen years his junior, brainy and cherubic, looked on with a calculation one could feel. Her clothes, flawless though plain, and the house, so ordered and spotless, symbolized American sobriety and respectability. Nothing admitted they dived off cliffs for a living.

Carl's laugh had been described as the sound of a car starting, and after hearing my predicament, he launched into a roaring grind. We blew into his office, decorated wall to wall with striking photos of parachuting and hang gliding. Still laughing, Carl ferreted out several photos of Norway's notorious Trollveggen Wall, gun metal gray and mile-high. By chance, he and Jean were soon to vacation there and Carl mentioned that the 5,600-foot wall had already recorded an established jump. Carl believed it could easily be bettered to world record height should we climb to the very top of the summit ridge, believed to be some 400 feet higher than the old site. Double checking topographic maps confirmed the record height. After Carl stated the jump's feasibility and their readiness to accomodate my schedule – for a whopping fee, of course – I had a strong hankering for a scotch. But not here! They'd take no drink, and their house stood dry as chaff in the thresher. Whatever, the whole deal seemed a windfall. The Trollveggen had the reputation of being Europe's biggest cliff, a face featuring scores of notorious rock climbs.

Once done with the filming, I'd have my pick of big routes – a boon, I thought.

We'd leave in three days – little time to assemble the tonnage of required gear. I visited the Boenish home twice more during the next few days. Carl emerged as the most singular individual I had ever met, heard about, or dreamed about. As Carl would rake through a garage full of gear, we'd talk – or rather he'd preach – about hang-gliding, then God, then BASE jumping, then literature. Suddenly, Carl's jaws would slacken, and he'd dash to his piano to butcher some classical refrain, just to jump back into conversation. And I can't swear I fully understood anything Carl ever said. His drift admitted his mixed bag of studies, from electrical engineering to classical music to quantum mechanics – all galvinized by a goofy mix of mysticism and personal revelations, coupled with the cryptic tenets of a religious system I could not quite discern. Often he would draw upon all the aforementioned, sometimes in the same sentence. His phrasing would vex Proust and his habit of citing theoretical examples would confuse even himself, for often their import had nebulous bearing on an already vague theme. It was no wonder our producer thought he was on LSD, or something stronger. I considered writing him off as a kook, but his laugh and genuine compassion were so disarming I always found myself laughing and excited. I respected him not so much as a doer of the outlandish as a man of heart, however inscrutable. I never expected to really know the man. Somehow, we met our schedule. Switching locations would prove simple, for the production team currently traveled in Europe, and swinging over to Norway promised to be easy compared to gaining Baffin Island, another continent away.

•

I hooked up with Carl and Jean in London and we flew to Oslo together. The national airlines were on strike, which left us to wad eight duffle bags into a rental car and head for Trondheim, eight hours north. The narrow road meandered through green valleys laced with swift alpine streams, glinting under the midnight sun. Somber clouds snarled and boiled off the frosted peaks above us. When we stopped for beers (sodas for Carl and Jean), I noticed the date, 1509, chiseled on the hearth. The sun dozed as Carl hit his second wind, launching into his most daring and absurd drift yet. The moment he seemed clear, he'd touch upon something so foreign that even Jean – usually mute – would laugh. Eyes focused on some distant quasar, Carl seemed wonderfully outrageous.

We crept into the sleepy town of Andalsnes, hedged on all sides by cliffs, cloud covered and mile high.

•

The next day we rise early and chug up a zigzag road to the highest path, then set out on a grueling march for Trollveggen's summit. We're joined by Fred Husoy, a young and dapper local climber whose intimate knowledge of the area will figure prominently in locating our record site. We shoulder packs and start humping up wet slabs and shifty moraines toward a snowy col. Carl hikes so slowly I finally take his pack, but halfway up a second scree slope he is again well behind. Fred dons his waterproof against an increasing drizzle, insisting on speed lest we lose visibility and the day to storm and clouds. We slog ankle-deep through a snowfield. When Carl catches up, wet clouds drape everything. By now I'm convinced Carl is the laziest adventurer to ever stand in boot leather. No amount of coaxing can quicken his pace. Finally, a little stone hut twenty minutes shy of the summit ridge offers a welcome roof from the noon shower.

Carl limps in and when he pulls up a pant leg, my jaw drops. Just above the ankle, his leg takes a shocking jag before rejoining his shin, two inches off plumb. It is remarkable he can even hike with such a limb, and I feel abashed to have pushed him. Fred stops wringing his wool hat to stare, dumbstruck. "Jesus, Carl, when did that happen?" Explaining that his leg had snapped in a hang-gliding accident several years back, Carl laughs through an exposition of his sapling and deerskin notions of natural healing. Some of his bewildering religious allusions come into focus: Christian Science. While everyone is dealt ample pain and suffering, Carl wants more, owing to a principle. "Shit, Carl," I whine, "an orthopod could surely fix that – it's hideous." No way. No doctors. Carl dismisses the lot with a laugh, his face wincing. When he pulls up his sock, his hands tremble from the pain . . . and Carl becomes all the more baffling.

When the shower outside eases, we plod up steep, snowy slabs toward the summit ridge – a mile-log dinosaur's back of pinnacles, clefts, and precarious boxcar blocks. Off the jagged ridge, the wall drops 5,600 feet to the Trondheim Valley. Behind, the rubbly slabs angle down several hundred feet to a high glacial plateau where perpetual snow rings an eerie lake of aquamarine, like a blue eye staring. Piebald clouds mask the ridge, making it difficult to decipher our location. Without Fred's knowledge of key landmarks, we'd wander blind.

We gain the ridge as the clouds momentarily part. It's fantastic to lie belly-down and stick our heads over the vast drop. As the clouds converge, Carl sets to rubbing his ankle, laughing, grimacing, then explaining his requirements. The wall beneath his launch must overhang, and it must remain overhanging for hundreds of feet, long enough to reach terminal velocity, for only at top speed can his lay-out positioning create enough horizontal draft for him to track – actually fly out and away from the wall to pop the chute in snag-free air. The further from the wall, the safer, for the new parachutes don't simply drop vertically, but glide four feet forward for every one foot down. It is not unheard of for a twisted line to deploy a chute backwards, leading the jumper into, not away from the cliff. With a laugh and full-moon eyes, Carl says, "Here, that would be fatal." He peers over the lip, chuckles, then looks back at us. "Fatal."

Just to our left, the spectacular, 200-foot Stabben Pinnacle cants out over the lip like a tilted smokestack. The spire's top projects forty feet out over the void. An exit there would prove far safer than leaping straight off the lip. Carl hangs tight as Fred and I climb up the soaking Stabben to start rock tests, the only true gauge of how far the wall drops vertically below. On terrain that is fractured and loose, we wobble a trash-can-sized boulder to the lip and roll it off. Five, six . . . Bam! Sounds like a mortar! "No good," laughs Carl. Way too soon to impact. The rocks continue rattling down for an astonishingly long time. We try again. This time I lean over the lip and watch the rock whiz downward, swallowed in fog 300 feet below. Three, four, . . . Bam! My head snaps up. Must be a jutting ledge just below the fog line. "Whatever, Stabben won't do," yells Carl. "It'd be crazy . . . ." The flinty smell of shattered rock lofts up just as it starts pouring.

Fred and I huddle in a snug alcove, but it's no use, so we stride for the valley while lightning cracks. Carl crawls slowly behind.

Twice more Fred and I explore the summit ridge, dashed by hailstorms – despite clear air space in the valley. It's aggravating. Trollveggen seems to create its own storms. The film producers, watching the rain wash their budgets, are wont for particulars, more so results, and my inability to even say where we'll jump from is considered impotence on my behalf. There is urgency to jump and be done with it, as Norway is the end of the production schedule, and the crew is looking toward Paris, the Greek Islands, or home. On the fourth scout, after a nasty piece of traversing that requires several rappels, we locate what we know is the highest possible exit the ridge affords. But again, rain and wind drives us off before we can start rock tests.

Now we're back, with clear skies, and the entire ridge is terrifically visible, zagging down on either side. We're definitely on the apex, walking freely on a made-to-order, ten- by-fifty foot ledge terminating in an abyss so ghastly that even Spencer Tracy would go for another rope. Lashed taut to three separate lines, I set feet on the lip, bend over the void and start lobbing off bowling-ball-sized rocks while Fred times the free-fall. They whiz and accelerate something ferocious, seem to fall forever, clean from sight. Twelve, thirteen . . . Fred and I trade amazed looks. This could do it! Seventeen, eighteen . . . BANG! A puff of white smokes near the base, thousands of feet below. The echo volleys round the amphitheater, likewise our yelps. This is the record site! That rock just free-fell farther than Half Dome is high. Fred points out the original launch spot, a quarter mile left and 400 feet below. We're home free. I chuck another rock and we watch it wane to a BB. BANG! I inform Fred that if Carl and Jean don't fancy this site, he will have to jump. Briefly considering the drop, his face flushes and he lurches back from the lip. "I quit!" he chuckles. I try to fathom strapping on a chute and plunging off, but it's too bizarre to reckon; just gape down a vertical mile to the cars creeping along the road! One thing I clearly see is that from a climbing perspective, the Trollveggen is very poor: loose and shattered rock, discontinuous crack systems, and the lower reaches bombed with stone fall; all in all, it is a vertical rubble pile. We ascend our fixed rope, return across the traverse, then, with the good news, dash for the valley as the first drops fall.

Weather delays us another five days but helicopters are on standby, cameras loaded, every angle fixed, with all logistics figured to the minute. Meanwhile, journalists throughout Scandanavia have flocked to Andalsnes. The papers run full-page hyperbole hatched by a dogged group thirty strong, all vying for the scoop. Ever approached, pried, I point to Carl and Jean. Carl laughs, then lets fly his bedeviled babbling as journalists feign understanding but take no notes. Jean delivers in two sentences of cold, hard narrative, and the journalists return to ask me what the hell Carl had said. One writer takes to quoting Carl directly but finds the translation to Norwegian impossible. A big-time Oslo stringer – a stunning virago who could challenge the Pope's vows – works a different line, citing previous jumping tragedies and questioning the viability of something authorities are already reluctant about. Everyone slinks around. Rain falls. Tension grows. We all wait. With all the media hoopla, all the delays, the story explodes to national news. Norwegian television runs a nightly update that propels the jump into continental notice. The Oslo station has a video crew in town, so with a week's momentum, the whole production takes on the pomp and gossip of Hollywood – precisely what I'd hoped to avoid. The entire town stands by, anxious, this impatience a reminder to fretting producers that every day in limbo means thousands wasted. Suddenly there's a rush for what requires the most steadfast deliberation. Throughout, the Boenishes have been, and are, ready.

The weather breaks at 8:00 P.M., July 5, 1984, with everyone scambling, desperate to shoot something, even in bad light. In two hours, cameramen are choppered into position. In a tricky piece of flying, the pilot deposits Carl, Jean, Fred, and me in a tight notch in the summit ridge, just forty feet from the launch site. This avoids the traverse and rappels; I shudder to think of having had to get the Boenishes across. Clad in a flaming red jumpsuit, Carl paces with energy enough to charge a power plant, while Jean, ever poised, begins assiduous study of the launch site. I pitch off a rock that whistles down into the night. Others follow to verify my estimates, but devulge another hazard. "Sure, they drop forever," laughs Carl, "but they're never more than ten feet from the wall!" That leaves no margin for error. Should they not stick the perfect, horizontal free-fall position, if they should carve the air even slightly back tilted – head higher than feet – they will track backwards. Carl explains with his hands, one hand as the wall, the other for the jumper; and when his hands smack together, I cringe. Success will require the perfect jump. Such news sets me thinking, but this is a judgment call, and the decision is left to Carl and Jean. Jean seems confident but rolls more stones toward the lip. Approaching midnight, the light fades to dusk with the great stone amphitheatre stretching below, dark and foreboding. Suddenly, the radio coughs out: "Come on, Long, let's get on with it!" The crew is freezing and the director of photography has declared it almost too dark to film. "Hey," snaps Carl, momentarily lucid, "I'm in no hurry to jump off this cliff, screaming past those ledges at midnight!" I quote this verbatim into the radio, and people relax; we talk things over. Carl's gusto is undeniable – "I'm here, I'm jumping!" – so we go for Plan B. He'll make a practice jump while the camermen preview and assess the angles. The sky is flawless, so we probably have at least another eight hours of good weather. After Carl's trial jump, we will resume in a few hours when full light returns. As Carl dons his parachute, I try and capture his hyperactivity on film, but it's too dark to even pull a focus, though there's light enough to see fine with naked, though dilated eyes. I repack the Arriflex and turn to the drama before the jump.

"Ten minutes," says Carl, jaw working steadily, eyes bulbous, hands fidgety. Jean, ever relaxed, cinches the last straps. Cued by a week of front-page spreads, the road below is jammed with cars of the curious, headlights winking in 1:00 A.M. grayness, the concession shop a beehive. Everyone is looking a mile up except us, who peer a mile down into the vague contours of the valley. "Five minutes," squeaks Carl. He pulls some streamers from his pack, and leaning off the ropes, I lob them off. No wind. They fall straight down, shrinking to a blur after just clearing those ledges. Everything's set.

"One minute," says Carl in a pinched voice. He secures his helmet, then slides twitching fingers into white gloves. He follows a final pitched rock with porthole eyes, visualizing his line.

"Fifteen seconds," he gasps, unclipping the rope and stepping up to the lip. Horns sound below. I'm taut, tied off to four ropes, feet on the edge, with a panoramic view of it all. Carl's shoes tap like a rhythm machine, eyes lost below. Carl starts the countdown, which Fred mimics into the radio: "Four, three, two, one . . . ." He's away! Arms go out to stabilize, legs bend and straighten, and he plummets down, jumpsuit whipping like a sail. With roaring acceleration Carl passes the ledges with ten feet to spare, body wooooshing, ripping the air. At 1,000 feet his arms snap to his sides and he starts flying horizontally away from the wall, fifty, one hundred, one hundred and fifty feet, at one hundred and thirty miles an hour, now a red dot. Thirteen, fourteen, fifteen . . . Pop! His big yellow chute unfurls like a circus tent for a casual glide down to the crowd. The picture-perfect jump. "Okay, Fred," I laugh, incredibly relieved, "You're next. Hurry and gear up!" We laugh at that one.

Back at the hotel at 3:30 A.M., it's madness among gnashing producers, frantic journalists, film loaders, battery chargers, pilots, and hangers-on, all guzzling tankards of Espresso (club soda for the Boenishes), checking for clouds by the minute. Everyone is anxious to get back to the Trollveggen, film the jump, and clear out. (A chartered jet is gassed and awaits the crew once the filming is over, hopefully by noon.) At 4:30 I lay down for a few Z's, but I'm so charged with coffee and expectations that it's hard to even lie still; sleep is impossible.

In fabulous 6 A.M. light two helicopters angle up through deep blue skies and deposit us onto our respective positions. The chopper jitters, blades alarmingly close to stone as we hop out onto the summit ridge. In thirty minutes we're set. There's a camera on the ground, one on a distant ridge, and one in a helicopter one hundred feet out before us. Again I'm taut on ropes, off the lip, with a camera angle some would murder for. I've got another camera ten feet to the side, looking straight down. The Boenishes will both jump, a second apart; Jean first, with the camera looking back. Carl has a super-wide angle lens facing down. We're covered! With all the previous weeks needled down to the next minute, the thrill is formidable. So much waiting, so many hassles. "Two minutes."

Utterly composed, Jean wrestles into her rig and helmet, then gazes a last time over the lip, feeling the rock with her eyes while taking mental notes on the two ledges jutting out directly below. Carl skates around like spit on a griddle, unnerving me.

"One minute . . . ."

I start rolling camera as the Boenishes take position: Jean's toes are over the lip, then she steps one pace back; Carl rattles inches behind. Hundreds of cars and twice as many people jam a mile of highway below. The chopper grinds in the distance.

"Ten seconds!" yells Carl. Jean later wrote: "Eyes fixed on the horizon, I raise my arms into a good exit position. Then from behind, 'Three! . . . Two! . . . One! . . .' For an instant my eyes dart down to reaffirm one solid step before the open air. Go! One lunging step forward and I'm off, Carl right on my heels. Freedom! Silence accelerates into a rushing sound as my body rolls forward. I quickly realize that last downward glance has been an indulgence now taking its toll, for I roll past the prone into a head-down dive which takes me too close to the wall. The first ledge is rushing towards me as I strain to keep from flipping over onto my back."

Through the viewfinder I see Jean dive-bombing for the first ledge. I freak and rip away the camera to see her scream by, virtually feet from doom. "Wow!" shrieks Fred. Jean somehow arches back to prone, then at terminal velocity, her hands come back and the duo starts swooping away from the wall like hawks, shrinking to colorful specks, still flying out, two hundred feet out, still free falling, farther out. "Pull the chute!" I scream. Sixteen, seventeen: POP! POP! It's history! A world's record, no injuries. Cameramen rave over the radios, having captured the footage of a lifetime. Newsmen and bystanders swarm upon the Boenishes after their pin-point landing. The world topples off my shoulders and I'm done, exhausted.

It's all smiles and champagne back at the hotel. One camera-man claims he's got the most exciting footage in the history of television. Delays notwithstanding, the show has gone remark-ably smoothly, but jumpy producers are still scrambling to pack and clear out. The executive producer is so concerned about an accident that he seems psychotic over leaving lest something happen retroactively. In two hours, everyone's on board the charter, jetting for London. That is, everyone save me and the Boenishes – the latter to vacation (I'm led to believe), me to settle last accounts, and climb. Presently I'm interested only in sleep, but, owing to journalists, even that is impossible until deep into the night.

After changing my mind a hundred times in two weeks, I decide to climb the Trollveggen, that matchless trash heap, ever-scoured by rock fall – a terrible, if grandiose challenge. I don't plan to return, so like most inveterate climbers, I can't just blow off Europe's biggest cliff when it's right down the road. I reluctantly start sorting gear, racking up the bare minimum for a racehorse, one-day ascent. A quick rap on the door and in rushes Fred, harried and stressed. "Carl's been in an accident and it looks bad!" A car accident? When I'm told he had hiked up first thing this morning, and had jumped from Stabben Pinnacle no less, I refuse to believe it. "Impossible!" After the last two sleepless days, Carl would most assuredly be resting his bum leg, as he'd done after every previous bit of activity. Our production had caused such a ruckus that jumpers were dropping in from all over Europe; any accident had been theirs, not Carl's. No! Carl had hustled two local climbers to hike him up. One man who had witnessed Carl's accident currently shook and stuttered before us. His rising burst of bad English says the jump has gone anything but well. *Stabben?!* Had Carl not assessed the site as "crazy"? Fred shakes his head, while I struggle to contain my rage. As a free citizen, Carl could do as he pleased, but Stabben? I lay out a quick plan; Fred and the young guide would scramble for the police to summon the rescue chopper while I would race to the pull-out beneath the Trollveggen. I am soon dashing across peat bogs until in line with Stabben Pinnacle. I frantically glass the lower wall, nearly a mile away. The cliff does not rise straight from the ground; rather, it rambles 1,500 feet over steep, grassy slabs to rear vertically for 3,000 feet to Stabben and the summit ridge. Carl surely is marooned somewhere on the lower slabs, but I have glassed every inch and see nothing of his red parachute. Again, nothing. There! I see something unfurled and breeze-blown on a shaded terrace. For ten minutes the binoculars are frozen in my hands, waiting for some movement, even a twitch. I scream for Carl to stand and wave. Nothing. "Goddamn it, Carl . . . get up . . . signal . . . ." The red canopy billows gently from the updraft. "Carl! . . . ." I'm starting to shake. I consider climbing up to him until glassing the terrain, now certain that a full day's wet and treacherous climbing guards his perch. My palms run sweat as prickly heat works my neck. I pace in circles, like an idiot. What to do but tramp back to the car? Fred squeals up with a red face, exclaiming that we've got to gear up. The Navy chopper's airborne, and if any climbing's involved, we'll have to do it. We race to a grassy field surrounding the Grand Manor of an expatriate British lord. Local newsmen file in as the police chief arrives. Hardly a crank, "told you so, American," the chief is disquiet. A pall tumbles from gray clouds, while rude newsmen mumble around, occasionally stealing glances at me. I single out the most obnoxious one, walk over, get in his face, and stare hard. Right now, it's not beyond me to deck him from pure stress. The police chief lays a calm hand on my shoulder and we exit to the lord's house to discuss my findings. The part about no movement causes the chief to lower his head; I've never seen a man look so solemn. He cringes at the forthcoming call to Jean, a task I duck. He does it straightaway, hating it. The number is dialed, he breathes deep, back straightening. As he begins, tears flow from both eyes, despite stoic features and controlled voice. "I . . . very much regret to inform you that your husband has been in an accident . . . and . . . and, it doesn't look very good." This last detail is the bare truth, and takes courage to immediately admit. I go outside and get into my harness. By no means am I convinced Carl is dead, even seriously injured, so I tell everyone as much, confronting some with the news, almost yelling it, and they nod slowly. The newsmen shrink away into faint mist, speaking sparingly among themselves – now huddled under trees, waiting.

The whop! whop! of the giant rescue chopper ricochets up the valley. It lands like a typhoon, arching trees, buckling photographers, scaring all with its powerful thumping. Fred goes and I stay, stay to pace, mill, sweat, and shiver, standing in a T-shirt and staring straight up into the rain. I look at no one, think of nothing, vaguely aware of the chopper's hammering pitch in the distance. When it returns, the ambulance starts up, but pulls off empty when the chopper shuts down and the crew slowly files out, looking serious. Fred walks over and says nothing. Under the lenses of six photographers, I flee to the lord's house to get a grip. My mind races to make sense of what makes no sense. *Stabben?!* The household won't face me. My teeth grind from anger and helplessness. When the policeman grabs the phone to shatter Jean with the news, I know I'm a coward for not doing so myself, and instead walk out into the crisp Norse air and easier breathing. Everyone looks confounded, as this puts a twist on what thousands have been told to admire. The doctor requests that I go aboard to identify the body. "For what?" I beg. The doctor looks away, and then I know this whole ordeal spares no one. We walk through wet, knee-high grass toward the ship. Amber light glints off new puddles. The day seems strangely fantastic.

•

Two days later, Jean hikes up to Stabben Pinnacle to try and determine something. Conclusions drawn, she tromps the ridge to the original site and jumps to a perfect meadow landing.

Flint Hard
and Flawless

HALF A MILE UP a vertical wall in Yosemite Valley, a 250-foot tangerine bullet of granite fires into the sky: the Lost Arrow Spire. Strikingly bold in profile, its freestanding summit is the most classic in America. Mere yards left plummets Upper Yosemite Fall, topped only by Angel Fall in its free-fall plunge. Wind whipped, sun blasted, yet often misty, the Lost Arrow Spire flanks a timeless panorama, grist for a billion postcards. Like a celestial atoll, the spire's top is quintessential no-man's-land, clearly unobtainable.

The Lost Arrow Spire both terrified and enchanted Yosemite's first climbers, whose priority was to bag the most exhilarating summits. Ever since the first pitons were driven in Yosemite Valley, the Spire presented the ultimate prize. But in 1935 techniques were raw, and to even the best climbers the spire posed seemingly impossible logistics. While the Spire's summit and the nearby rim are roughly the same level, they are separated by a 100-foot wide cleft of mountain air. Someone could rappel the 200 feet into the notch between the spire and the main wall, but then what? The spire's inside wall looked dead blank and fearsomely overhung, and no climber was willing to stitch the spire with countless bolts. Climbers wanted to use fair means. A binocular view yielded only the faintest crack on the spire's outside face, and this vanished altogether some 40 feet from the top. In 1935 the only thin pitons were made of malleable soft iron, and potential climbers had to wonder if thin, taffy-hard pegs could find sufficient purchase in the scant seam. And what about the 40 foot blank stretch? They pictured themselves lashed to the rearing spire, tried to visualize the ghastly exposure – hundreds and thousands of feet of air beneath their boots – and the notion filled the knickers of every dreamer. Alternatives were discussed: the spire's girth is slim, but a 100-foot lasso seemed preposterous, a parachute landing too dicey, a catapult ludicrous, a cantilevered telephone pole all the more absurd.

Richard Leonard wanted a closer look. Only so much could be surmised with binoculars, so he and fellow members of Berkeley's Cragmont Climbing Club suffered the four-mile hump up the trail to the north rim. Leonard and others were fresh off the first ascent of the Cathedral Spires, inspired Yosemite routes that put the C.C.C. group at the apex of American rock climbing. As the men would soon realize, the fractured, mottled cosmetics of the Cathedrals contrasted sharply with the polished terror of the Lost Arrow Spire. From Yosemite Point, a hundred yards east of the spire, Leonard and company roped down airy slabs for a closer look. Said Leonard, "We obtained a view that was terrifying even to those who had climbed the Cathedral Spires. It was unanimously agreed we would never attempt it." Leonard would keep that promise, later stating that the Arrow proved "the nightmare of all those who have inspected it closely." But following the world war came a new generation, armed with fresh courage and refined equipment.

•

August 1946

One man's nightmare is another man's dream, and John Salathé had a dream: an angel told him he would make three historic climbs: The southwest face of Half Dome; The north face of Sentinel; and the Lost Arrow Spire. The 47-year-old Swiss blacksmith was new to climbing, but his stalwart constitution and mechanical savvy would help actualize his dreams, thus ushering in the era of big-wall climbing.

On that August day, Salathé was to meet friends on the rim. They never showed, so Salathé decided to rappel alone the 250 feet into the notch, thus becoming the first man to gain the spooky shade between the Spire and the rim. Salathé peered down the 1,000-foot gash that drops from the notch to the talus – a nasty collection of flared cracks and claustrophobic chimneys. The Lost Arrow Chimney had seen several tentative attempts in the thirties and clearly seemed a plum; but for now only the actual Spire interested Salathé. Spotting a small ledge at the notch's outer end, Salathé secured his white line to a stout block and started slithering out onto the Spire's breathtaking outside face. A climber later likened this to stepping out onto a window sill on the Empire State Building's hundredth floor. Ten feet out, Salathé found a small corner and patiently began banging pitons into the incipient crack. The blacksmith was not using the soft iron duds of Leonard's era, but custom jobs he had hand forged from Model-A axle stock. After 30 feet he gained a small ledge; and from the ledge's left margin, a second thin crack allowed him 40 feet of tenuous nailing to another ledge that now bears his name. As Steve Roper has aptly written, "His position on the outer face . . . was as wild and lonely as any Yosemite climber had ever experienced." With the shadows streaking across the wall, Salathé returned to the notch and ascended the dangling rope to the rim. For this, he enjoyed not the handy mechanical rope ascenders of today. Rather, he used prusik knots – nasty little slip knots pushed slowly and strenuously up the line.

The next week Salathé returned with San Francisco climber John Thune. They quickly regained Salathé's high point, where Salathé continued nailing up a left-curving crack for 80 desperate feet. But the cracks disappeared completely some 40 blank feet from the summit. Salathé immediately started drilling a ladder of bolts up the final headwall, but after only two, the diamond-hard rock so blunted his drills that they became useless. Realizing a tedious and time-consuming job would alone secure the top, Salathé and Thune retreated, rallied by their progress. Now knowing the necessary gear for a summit bid, they soon planned to return.

"Competition is the essence of sport and the spur to thought . . . ." So wrote Anton Nelson who, a week after Salathé's last effort, sneaked up to the rim with Jack Arnold, Fritz Lippmann and Robin Hansen. They hiked fast, for they had a plan more ludicrous than any in Yosemite's history. Hansen's forte wasn't climbing, but baseball; and the four had in mind that if Hansen could hurl a line over the Spire's rounded summit, a lunatic could ascend that line to the top. Hansen would pitch from the rim, winging a tethered weight the hundred feet out and over the Spire. The line would then snake down the Spire's exposed outer face – they hoped. Climbers in the notch could then edge out over the void, nab the free line, and ascend it to the summit. The plan sounded basic, but countless attempts saw the line slide off the domed summit and whizz through the defile. The four were not laughing at the cord's furious retreat, or the subsequent smack of the weight into granite, 100 feet below. But Hansen kept at it. Finally, in late afternoon, he threw the perfect strike. Weighted with marlin sinkers, the thin line slithered down to Salathé Ledge, just as planned.

Nelson and Arnold rappelled into the notch the next morning. They labored the whole day just to get to the first ledge, mauling their soft iron duds, cursing Salathé and his axle pegs. Embarrassed, frustrated, the pair retreated up to the rim, leaving a line fixed from the first ledge to the notch. They still had another 40 feet to reach Salathé Ledge, the one reached by the blacksmith three weeks earlier.

The following day Nelson and Arnold quickly regained the first ledge. But after absorbing several miserable pitons the crack pinched so tightly that no amount of blasting could set their soft iron. They could all but touch Salathé Ledge, yet were altogether stumped. Desperate, Nelson lassoed a tiny horn, then ordered Arnold to prusik the 20 feet to the ledge and the pitched line, still dangling 40 hours after Hansen's successful toss. Stout lines were pulled 150 feet up the sheer wall, then 100 feet across the gap to anchors on the rim.

Now, would they draw straws? No, for according to Nelson, "the stern code of the climber decrees that the lightest man shall lead doubtful pitches." What code? What decree? No, this is just impromptu jive, invented to preclude the corn-fed Nelson from going first. The stern code was news to Jack, pacing, cowering, chain smoking, and stealing sad glances at the rope, dangling in the breeze. It seems probable that Arnold spent the countdown blowing smoke in Nelson's face – a face smiling like a thief. Overcome with anxiety, Arnold frantically huffed three more cigarettes, then, according to one author, "placed his weight on the rope and moved upward on his lonely odyssey to the Arrow's summit."

While the saga of the tossed cord is common knowledge, it seems likely that few climbers of today realize the madness inherent in this stunt. The Spire's top is not so minuscule as it is rounded; mere wrinkles check a line held in place by the weight on the business end. Imagine a kite string draped over a bowling ball and you've got it. Arnold's 120-foot prusik ascent would provide him with ample time to mull his fate should the rope twang off the top. Fortunately, it did not; and at twilight Jack Arnold became the first man to stand on the most radical summit of the day. After planting a bomb-proof bolt anchor, he waited as Nelson prusiked up and the real fun began: a fearsome aerial Tyrolean Traverse – later to become an Arrow tradition.

After long hours of rope exchanges and re-anchoring, a taut line spanned from tip to rim, across the bottomless chasm. In total darkness Nelson checked his knots for the thousandth time, heaved a final sigh – then sent Jack Arnold across. Village lights twinkled a half mile below, but Jack's eyes were welded to the rim.

•

Labor Day, 1947

Salathé had been scooped . . . or had he? The Spire had succumbed to a mad rope shenanigan and technically was no longer virgin. But no one claimed the Arrow had actually been climbed, not traditionally anyway. The climbing community had to acknowledge Jack Arnold's feat, but no one was queuing up to repeat it. Meanwhile, Nelson passionately defended his tactics, claiming that after but three ascents, the Spire's initial cracks were irreversibly thrashed, never again to allow passage. Concerning his rope trick, Nelson concluded that, "it was in effect an admission of the Arrow's unclimbability." Nelson would have all believe these were the Spire's own words; but Salathé heard different voices. He knew the controversy dealt only with the actual Spire; the 1,000-foot Arrow Chimney below was still unclimbed. Arnold et al. had bagged the summit by excluding 80 percent of the climb – like starting at 25,000 feet on Everest. John Salathé would clear the air.

Partnered by the ubiquitous Anton Nelson, Salathé commenced war with the nasty gash angling vertically to the notch, 1,000 feet above. In the next four-and-a-half days they encountered the most difficult climbing yet accomplished in America: squeeze chimneys, loose bulges, guillotine flakes. The cracks were often too wide for their pitons, obliging Salathé to risk long falls between inadequate protection. Anticipating long blank sections, Salathé had fashioned a diminitive sky-hook. Lashed to a long, thin rod, this allowed terrifying progress over otherwise inviolate stone. Ledges were few and the pair endured several sleepless nights hanging from ropes. Worse still, blast-furnace heat and scant water combined for the bleakest privations. Once they finally oozed onto the notch, the mighty Spire awaited. Salathé slowly reached his high point (attained with John Thune the previous August). Facing the "flint hard and flawless" headwall that Nelson would later wax verbose about, Salathé set off, Nelson lashed hard to the most stupendous location in Yosemite. In the waning light of day five, Salathé punched home the eighth and final bolt, stepped from his aid slings, and frictioned up the conical summit to the top.

•

September 1964

Frank Sacherer and Chuck Pratt gaze up the long dark gash of the Lost Arrow Chimney. Packs are light, for they plan to climb the entire chimney in one day – all free. Both men are counted among the world's premier climbers, unofficial titles wrought from free climbing big routes formerly done with aid – aid from pitched ropes, aid from hooks strapped to long steel rods, aid from nylon stirrups clipped into a string of iron pitons. These techniques still prevail when necessary, and it is up to folks like Sacherer and Pratt to prove when it is not. Climbing has evolved from pure nerve to athletics, and the vogue is to free climb with hands and feet on available features – at almost any cost. Just gaining the top no longer seems enough. It's a matter of style. After a full day's battle, Sacherer and Pratt collapse onto the notch, spent, but champions of their plan. Sacherer later said "You'll never be so tired as the day you free climb the Lost Arrow Chimney in one day." Now, only the actual Spire had any aid left.

•

August, 1984

Dwight Brooks (D.B.), Bob Gaines, and I pant about the notch's shattered blocks, tortured by the overhead sun, scrambling to find a decent anchor. We're anxious, charged for an all-out effort. It's Bob's idea, and while we all concede the Spire's status, only Bob thinks we can free climb the whole thing. To our knowledge, no one has made a completely free ascent, so the thrill of the pioneer amplifies everything. But wait. Though we hiked to the rim last night and rose at dawn, a Slavic team has somehow slipped in before us and the threesome is currently on the first lead – doing things I've never seen before. The leader wields a geologist's hammer and climbs in his underwear. We must accord them some time to get well above, but it's murderous pacing in this heat. Our desire is uncontainable.

Finally D.B. cinches the rope round a block; I further clip it through an in situ peg. Bob tiptoes out a brief ledge, his heels now half a mile above the Valley floor, his fingers plugging a wee crack in the recess of a thin corner. His feet start stemming on the corner's off-set walls; his outside hand palms hot orange granite while his inside hand claws the mere crease in the corner. A side pull, a high step, and Bob's got it: the first pitch.

We follow. It's tough, and the wall drops off like the world's edge. Snug on the three-by-ten ledge, we re-con the overhanging crack leading to Salathé Ledge, a strenuous 40 feet above. As D.B. arranges the belay, Bob re-racks the gear. I bathe my hands in chalk and mop my brow. It's hot! Bob hands me the sling of gear, cracks a smile, and I take off. Hands plug deep in the flared crack, where aggressive jamming meets Salathé Ledge, distended like a ship's prow over a vertical sea of granite. This marks the high point of Salathé's solo reconnaissance; it is also the spot where the maniac Arnold began prusiking the tossed cord. Bob eyes the summit, 120 feet above; D.B. scans the main wall, 150 feet away; I gaze at the Valley floor, two counties below. All eyes meet, flabbergasted at the prospect of ascending a pitched line from here. Forget it!

D.B. moves left on holds soon to run out. The blue rope hangs free from the sheer wall. Now a dilemma: the only protection is a one inch aluminum block bashed into a pocket, its sling faded and denuded. A good nut will fit, but only where his fingertips are barely slotted. He sighs, clips the trashy sling, steps his feet up to his hands and starts madcap liebacking – hinging out, then back, then out again. I look away. Feeding out blind inches of rope, my eyes zoom down, down to the Valley floor. Weekend traffic honks along at a clogged but steady clip, each car with exclusive moves, yet all part of one continuous flow. Eyes pan up to the ledge to D.B., now with one leg dangling, the other hooked above his head. His fingertips are maxed on oblique crystals; his wide eyes are both focused and lost in the function. Sweat flies off a flurry of limbs. Bob and I swap looks, only to glance back at D.B., now crooked in the most outlandish attitude – hands crossed, neck craned, feet pawing on nothing. Still, he moves up. We scream encouragement, the echo reporting off the main wall. D.B. now pumps up a good crack to the hanging stance beneath the last lead, a ladder of bolts up the flint hard and flawless headwall. D.B. hangs free from the anchor and his silhouette on the vertical plug is spectacular.

A thousand gasps later and we're all assembled, cloistered round one bolt, hanging in the most exotic place in Yosemite. We're clinging to the Spire like gnats on a flagpole. There's an old sling threaded through the bolt. I untie it, nudge Bob, extend my arm and let her fly. With amazement we watch it slowly waft down to the talus, never touching the orange face. We feel every inch of the wall below. No one's yawning.

My eyes close and my head leans against the rock. A steady drip of sweat splashes onto my legs. The sun-wicked fall is just an ivory ribbon, turning to mist 1,000 feet below. The air is dead, suffocating. Still, I'm not budging till calm and settled, a vain plan at THIS mooring. Regardless, the Slavs are still wrestling with the Tyrolean exit, and if perchance I can free the headwall, I want to gain a vacant summit.

It's time. Boots are laced till the grommets bend. D.B. secures the belay; Bob pockets his lens cap and smiles: "Do it!" Twenty feet pass moderately on sharp holds. I clip the rope through an ancient bolt and with several thin moves gain a thick, down-hanging flake. Underclinging allows a survey of the bulging crux. It's flint hard, but there's a flaw – a shallow, bottomless V-slot above that looks to have a good lip.

The move into the slot is made using the last half inch of my index finger. Another savage yank. Feet now stemmed on the slot's opposing walls and then slowly buttering off. Some frantic wiggling of fingertips into a dinky lock, limbs shaking with strain. Can't hang here long but there's not even a dimple for my feet. "I'm gonna rip! . . . ."

"No! Try something . . . anything . . . we've got you," they yell, not about to accept me falling off without trying something rash. Here goes. I place my foot on zero and lunge for the lip. Some lip! Feels like a greased beach ball. I hang it momentarily, then . . . ping! Slamming down on a Salathe bolt, I get lowered quickly to the belay.

The electric spook, the tiny cars, the heat – all gone. All that's left is the craving to succeed. But how? Sipping the last water, we discuss alternative moves, for the lunge is just too ridiculous. Off again, soon cranking back into the slot and again wiggling fingertips into that dinky pocket – kid stuff compared to the next stretch. I must try something different here. Palm off the left wall, pinch a wafer edge, stem feet on precious little and gingerly stretch over the slot. The tendons in my finger will explode should I tax them further on that wafer. Gamble that feet will briefly stick and match hands on the beach ball; shuffle feet up on other smears. No holds, no purchase, only the friction of boots and hands. Above, the Spire angles off 20 feet to the top, but mantling over the bulge feels horrific.

"You've got it!" they scream.

"The hell I do . . . watch me!"

Elbow is cocked, palm down and pressing . . . hand greasing off . . . high step onto the beach ball, foot starts sliding . . . palm slides to the last inch, foot too shaky for weight transfer – it's move or plummet.

"Crack it!" The echo agrees.

Right hand instinctively blurs up . . . slap! – bucket. It's a done thing! Fifteen easy feet and the summit's mine, 38 years after Jack Arnold. Not until tying off the bolts do I realize my whole body is running sweat, clothes *and* boots soaked through. The moves are fairly hard, but the real battle is with the heat. Later, while securing ropes to the rim, Bob comments that this whole venture seems like an hallucination.

"It ain't over yet," I laugh, clipping into the taut line and zipping out over the defile.

This is It!

INSTANTLY, INEXPLICABLY, the atmosphere explodes. Yuccas arch; vision is a whirl of sandblasting gravel and slipstreamed cacti. As I crash to the ground and cover my head, my heart stops. Who hasn't seen the films: the tornado winds, the spiraling mushroom. I know this heralds a thousand-megaton bomb. In a second, an otherworldly whine rises from a whisper to a deafening roar. I press my ears until my skull flexes. A whooshing vortex sets me rolling . . . over and over.

This is it! Just as fast, the din fades into the horizon, leaving me balled and covered in debris. Stunned, I quickly unfold, gain my hands and knees, and stare out into the desertscape. I make out a fleeting black object, but it's now miles off. The impression that it is only 100 feet off the ground convinces me I'm still seeing stars.

•

Another few gulps and the quart's a pint. Whew! It is only 9:30 and the mercury's already pushing 100 degrees. My big blue company car bombs on toward Joshua Tree. Banking on good tunes and a cool cabin, I had intentionally nabbed this massive luxury model, only later to realize both the radio and air conditioner are broken. The remaining club soda sails down and I grab another bottle.

We are slated to start filming at Joshua in six weeks. Our plans entail breaking countless park regulations, so I've chosen to negotiate personally with the Park Superintendent, hoping to bluff through on professional pretense. My dress clothes lie in the trunk, neatly starched and pressed. Sweat soaked, I writhe in the front seat, my gym trunks drenched and my sunglasses steaming up. Worse, I've picked up some funk rash in Asia and it's irresistible to claw my neck when the sweat rolls down – which is continuous. Venturing the three hours to Joshua without the chance to climb is maddening, but in June, the domes are wicked hot. My boots are aboard anyhow.

At the military town of Twentynine Palms, I swing into a market for more water. Heat waves waft off the desert and the dusty streets are vacant. I consider slipping the butcher a fin for a stint in the meat locker. I grab two bottles of seltzer. The young cashier wants to talk but grows silent after noticing something on my neck. A mongrel pants at the store entrance, his tongue so slack it looks like a barber's strop. I stumble out into the swelter and pan over to the military base. Fenced in by triple barbed wire, sentries mope around in varying states of dispair. A news clip on the store's outside bulletin board states the new base security procedures: No civilians whatsoever; and any plane entering restricted air space will be "aced." They're sitting on something I'll never see.

As my car rolls into Park Headquarters, I chug the remaining seltzer and roll the cool bottle on my neck. And to think of having to work in this hellhole, watching the chollas grow . . . . Someone so marooned must hold their job, and its duties, in bitter contempt. Hope the superintendent is otherwise. A quick change of clothes and a sprint to the office. Their air conditioner also doesn't work, and the inmates look like my four-door Lincoln is parked on their toes. The super curtly shakes hands, then dashes behind his desk, a huge fan humming six inches before his face. When he talks, or rather barks, it's straight through the fan and he sounds like an alien. After I give a brief rundown of our filming plans, the super shakes his jaded head and asks me what the hell's on my neck. A real snapper, this guy. But look, there's a picture of the super climbing, and a sling of old soft-iron pegs. The drift shifts to climbing. I leave an hour later, soaked, but with a special permit to break the rules.

Relieved, I drive back via the Monument, swilling all kinds of water. As the company bomb rolls into Hidden Valley Campground, the urge is overpowering. The brake is set, the boots go on, then some hot-footing to the "White Rastafarian," a half mile off, but shady. I reckon to do some bouldering prior to soloing even easy stuff. After one problem it becomes obvious that, while one can climb, it is utter misery in this heat. Forget it! I start pacing back to the car, a quarter mile of open desert before me. From habit, eyes scan the ground as feet shuffle through a maze of barbed shrubs. Then, barely perceptible, a shadow darts cross my path. Or did it . . . .

•

Now on my feet, I blink and squint, trying to confirm or dismiss this screaming black phantom. As my heart starts back up, a second shape silently rockets by but 100 feet overhead. The speed is so awesome that it seems more of a sensation than a corporeal image. It is well in the distance before focus is possible. As the sound waves catch up and the sand begins to riot, I note something peculiar and vow to stay standing, staring. No way! When a massive chunk of metal strafes the desert's skin at mach whatever, the surface revolts with such overwhelming violence that every man goes down, period. The sound could shatter a bowling ball and the gusts could strip a knight of armor. I clutch my ears, crash to the ground, and start rolling. In a moment the fury's past and I'm again on my feet, squinting through streaming eyes. My ears buzz, my head rings, but, yes, there's something odd all right: that jet is upside down, mere feet off the ground, at 1,000 plus miles per hour. Closing on Ryan Mountain, it angles up five degrees, rights itself with a half twist, then arcs straight up into the naked sky.

Dream On, Irian Jaya

by Dwight Brooks and John Long

DWIGHT: WE FLEW A THOUSAND MILES past Jayapura, the capital of Irian Jaya, to Jakarta. Both of us (John Long, an historic crossing of Borneo behind him, and myself, heading to remote Indonesian locales for the fourth time) were well aware of the bureaucracy involved getting permission to enter the unexplored areas of Irian Jaya, Indonesia's most troubled province, and ethnologically the most primitive place on earth. If you don't have a Jakarta-issued rag of paper called a Surat Jalan, you can't even enter Irian, let alone catch a bush plane to Wamena, where mountain (as opposed to swamp) fun begins. While astronomical sums might part the bush for a full-scale expedition, they are no guarantees of free and easy access. In 1984, for example, a large American film crew was shipped out on arrival, in spite of approval from Jakarta, due to expanded efforts by the Indonesian military (ABRI) to "pacify" various reactive mountain tribes, angered into battle upon being informed they were no longer Him-Yals, or Sibilers but "Indonesians". We learned that rather than try to bribe every soldier we met, being polite, patient and most importantly, fluent in Indonesian were the most effective tools for covering ground. On the other hand, tourists have been shot at, and journalists have been shot, but most of those people acted clumsily, or foolishly, around soldiers, and by the time muzzles barked they knew why.

No matter what your Irian itinerary may be, you must enter through Jayapura, formerly Sukarnapura, Hollandia, and Kota Baru. It has degenerated shockingly since the Dutch were manipulated out in the early sixties, and this no thanks at all to a bungled ABRI para-drop, which saw hundreds of soldiers dead from cannibals, disease and starvation, and not one Dutch casualty. This once-idyllic tropical nugget is now a floundering coastal outpost, where most civic amenities are defunct and decay is the rule. Transmigrants from other provinces funnel in, asserting a "hereditary" right to Melanesian West New Guinea which stems from the marginal control exercised on its coasts by the Tidore Sultanate in the seventeenth century. Raw sewage flows in the streets, Manado prostitutes abound, buildings are either patched up with rusting tin or engulfed by jungle, and the military presence is strenuously pronounced.

With no reservations we left this sweltering commode for Wamena (Wam = pig, ena = I have: pigs are the paramount symbol of wealth in New Guinea). Wamena is a scenic mountain village in the famous Baliem Valley which has become increasingly accessible to tourists.

Once-feared Ndani warriors, naked save for the penis gourd, or koteka, stare absently, ask for cigarettes, and gladly agree to porter loads for smokes or crumply red dime-value notes. Fifteen years ago they sat atop 40-foot bamboo watchtowers, scoped raiding parties, and met them in battle with fifteen-foot lances. Warfare once defined power structures, and payback raids insured economic stability; but today such activities are brutally suppressed by ABRI with bullets, burning of villages and, reportedly, torture. Old ways persist in some areas, however, and the cordillera running through Irian Jaya features a staggering array of valleys, ravines, caves, sinkholes, and forests that far exceeds, at present, the administrative capacities of the government.

Stone-age people still exist in certain parts of Irian Jaya, and There is a broad range of acculturation. Some have seen airplanes and electric goods and are quite accustomed to them. Others have seen these things but think they are forms of magic. Still others have seen white men or Indonesians only occasionally and are very unsure what they are. In a few torturously-isolated places it is still possible to make a first contact. John and I were lucky in this regard because we applied rock climbing skill to jungle-shrouded limestone, giving us access to remote plateaus and sinkholes. These plateaus and sinkholes, densely green from the air and too airy for foot patrols were the best bet. We looked for hunter-gatherers who move their villages frequently, and who are never seen unless they want to be. Neither of us knows where, exactly, the most primitive places we reached are. We could guess within a map grid, but we have sworn to each other to clam up, for obvious reasons. We travelled light and fast with hunters who meandered extravagantly through excruciating bush for weeks. We spent nights in many obscure places: caves, trees and declivities where wide-eyed inhabitants occasionally regarded us as other-than-human.

We had tremendous luck making friends with many people who weren't sure whether we were ancestors or ghosts. Maybe it was because whenever we got somewhere we opened the packs and gave things away: food, tobacco, medicine. My best guess is that they picked up immediately what a charge we got from seeing them in the first place. They like that. All vibe. We were big, we could hike as fast as they could, we chewed plenty of betel nut and we laughed a lot. No big deal – most of the time.

Trekkers wander the Baliem and some go to Illaga to climb the Dolomitic Puncak Jaywijaya, but few engage in systematic deviation from the maze of central tracks linking the various large villages of the massif. Traveling with the locals on their own circuitous routes, doing things their way, allows you that lateral sense that will position you for discoveries. Usually in big villages there will be an Indonesian administrator who'll direct you along as well as pointedly dissuade you from going to certain areas. What worked for us was to go, discreetly, right to the most forbidden area and start from there.

Irian is awesomely large, and the topography is riddled with deceptive features, places where aboriginal people can live undisturbed. No worries. If you are willing to take the time to confront the hazards involved, you may win the confidence of someone who will slash routes over dozens of 10,000 foot ridges, share bugs with you for food, pick a tenuous descent down a limestone face, slide down lianas into a sinkhole, and point out a hidden village. Usually, there is a sort of password for each region. You shout it out. If it is shouted back, you're in. If not, you run – we did both. Grim things can happen, obviously, but it isn't likely, unless you chop down a papaya tree or kill a pig. The guys you're with will read the bush signs, maddeningly subtle ones that say, "Come on," or "Shove off."

Our first "first contact," twenty-two days out of Wamena, was with a group of Uhundunis, who had heard about white people, but had never seen them. After each male had pinched our skin to ensure we were there, we watched them hack up a giant cassowary, a flightless bird whose talons are quite capable of disembowelling a man. In order to communicate with the various tribes, we had accumulated interpreters as we progressed. To greet an Uhunduni is not simple: Justinus, our Ndani friend, could speak to Itthips, a Woogi. Itthips was conversant in Jinak, and so spoke a good deal more with Ekjinak than Justinus could ever dream of. Ekjinak however, spoke no Uhunduni, nor did Ombaipufugu, who did indeed speak Jinak. Without the bilingual Ombaipufugu we wouldn't have been able to express our good intentions to the band of Uhundunis. That might well have precluded this writing. As it went, they sacrificed the cassowary on our behalf, and proved hospitable, though guarded. They didn't so much cook the stringy meat as draw it slowly over the fire. I was uncertain about this. Not so John, who was in the throes of severe hunger and hovered over Chief Kabatuwayaga and his minions as they apportioned servings. A premature reach for the banana leaf on which his serving lay nearly cost him his hand, which was blocked by a swift stone ax stroke. They screamed and jumped about, getting very clearly across that he should wait just a moment. Scarcely deterred because he was starving, John squatted back and looked on with marked determination. Then Chief Kabatuwayaga summoned his sorcerer, Tebegepkwekwe. Tebegepkwekwe smiled at John benignly, and spoke to Ombaipufugu. Our four interpreters put their heads together and Justinus explained in Indonesian that Tebegepkwekwe wished to reassure John that he knew John hadn't intended to reach for the food. Surely he wouldn't have been so reckless. A mogat, or major bush spirit had impelled his hand, and if it seized him again Tebegepkwekwe volunteered sterner measures to ensure it would leave him alone, so long as John didn't mind being suspended upside-down with thick blue smoke purifying his head. Tebegepkwekwe declared the mogat had probably been following us for days, and asked if we'd bathed in the bend of any river. Well, we had, actually. There we were; he rested his case. Then Tebegepkwekwe withdrew from a snakeskin sheath an eight-inch cassowary quill with a tiny white egret feather lashed to the tip. Feverishly he waved the quill over each serving. None of the Uhundunis could believe we didn't know what he was doing. Of course, it finally came through: lesser spirits, sulumilewolebalabats, must be carefully shooed away from the food before it would be safe to eat.

Instead of eating a second portion, as John did, I asked Justinus to find out where they got their axe-heads, which were made of a deep blue stone. Eventually it was explained that several times a year they met Monis, with whom they traded women for blades. The usual price was six for one, and I haven't the heart to spell out which went for which. Apparently the axe-heads were obtained swimming among fish in a secret stream, whose location was jealously guarded. We were fortunate that a Moni was then among them. The terrible scars he had on his knees and ankles from the adzes that had slipped his grasp validated his claim.

JOHN: After fourteen years of continuous adventuring I remained convinced that nothing could surprise me, that I'd seen all things bizarre. But when the Uhunduni chief waved a plume over the victuals, I stood (or rather squatted) corrected. Whereas we'd seen much, they'd seen little, and what we brought seemed as novel to them as their arrow wounds, kotekas, and sweet potato diet seemed to us. After this feather business we decided to hang – for a while anyway – with the Uhundunis, certain we would experience things stranger than fiction, and quite so. On the second night we produced the Coupe de Ville – the Walkman. Under the feeble rays of the cooking shack's little fire, a handful of tribesmen marveled and balked over the Bic lighter as Dwight (D.B.) and I searched for just the right tape. We decided on a searing jazz/fusion number, plugged it in, cranked it up, then slipped the little headphones over the chief's pierced ears. His eyes popped wide, filled with tears, and his features screwed up. Then he fell into such a paroxysm that I quickly nabbed the headphones lest we be assaulted for attempting sorcery on the chief. But the chief's peers felt otherwise, for one instantly wrenched the tape deck from my grasp, slipped on the phones, and commenced pawing and slapping at himself in a ludicrous fashion. Another donned the phones and broke into a singular version of jungle scat singing. Twenty other warriors jumped about with uncontainable curiosity, anxious to get their turn. The chief continued ranting. The scene escalated to a near riot. Impatient natives crowded around the listener as veterans babbled loud and long. Suddenly, there was a shriek and panicked tribesmen dove for the exit, damn near bringing down the grass hut. The eyes of the current listener bulged like a catfish, due in some part to the volume having been cranked up to 10! He droned and screamed, both hands clutching his adze, which he swang willy nilly, splintering this, shattering that. Then he rose off his haunches, twirling his tool at speed, screaming, limbs quaking, face seized with excitement, fear. The remaining tribesmen didn't bother with the tiny horseshoe exit, now logjammed with diving black bodies. They simply blasted headlong through the hut's thick grass siding. This decimated the shack's superstructure but did nothing to check the hatchet of the crazed Uhunduni. Fiendish howling poured forth as firelight seeped through the hut's exits, outlining two dozen jumpy Uhunduni's whose glassy eyes alternated between the sacked hut . . . and us. We squirmed, but our four interpreters were fit to vomit for stress and anguish, their heads lowered and shaking, lips quivering. "I think we go now . . . I think we go now," volleyed about in the rising inflections of four languages. Suddenly, with the crack of adze to wood, the shack shifted wildly left, then collapsed, the Uhunduni jazzman groping free just before the parched roof burst into flames. The resulting bonfire provided more than adequate light to study the two dozen glowing Uhunduni faces that showed what no man can describe.

Justinus had good reason to tremble, as the Uhundunis had been traditional enemies of his clan. He knew that I had already affronted the chief by grabbing food prior to having the ghosts exorcised. Now I had caused the chief's emotional collapse and precipitated the sacking of the communal cooking hut. Soon we faced the chief, who fingered the bright yellow Walkman while his teary eyes burned holes through us. He wanted some answers! First, who was responsible for cramming all those people into the tape deck? Second, how did he know those imprisoned were not the souls of his dead relatives? Third – and this he voiced with dreadful gravity – *who* had tortured those souls enough to make their voices sound like the damned?

To be accused of torturing the souls of the chief's dead kin put us in a position of considerable concern. The chief and our four interpreters carried on for a time, they always aquiescing to the chief's thunderous speech. Once the chief's drift trickled down to Justinus, we had great difficulty understanding his pidgen Indonesian and pre-cambrian English. Justinus wisely capitalized on this, telling the chief it would take all night to explain the question and decipher an answer. The chief wouldn't give us all night, but he would wait until the moon was overhead. With a mile-long face he ordered us to our assigned hut to work on some answers. We quickly exited past many savage eyes. One hundred yards away lay our hut – luckily isolated – whence we pitched non-essentials and cinched the straps on our now feather-light packs. Ekjinak snatched up a narrow stone and began filing his canines, perhaps anticipating an end-all effort of self defence. Rent through with terror, Itthips spastically hopped about in a cross-legged position, probably to avoid the arrow trees Uhun-dinis are said to be able to make spring from the ground.

"I think we go now!" shouted D.B.

"We're gone!" I added, shouldering my pack. "I don't want the chief waving no egret feather over me!" As the chief's pad roared with argument, we slunk into the darkness, at first like Hindus on hot coals and later like Carl Lewis. We hit the faint trail at full stride, reversing by daybreak what previously had taken three grueling days.

In all likelihood, we could have redressed our crimes with some form of payback, the value of which might not have exceeded those things we dumped from our packs. D.B. joked that at worst we would have had to sacrifice Justinus, but little humor registered on that native's face, a face anxious to put further miles behind us.

We gained the Sungai Pit (Sungai = river), and this we followed to its confluence with the great Sungai Baliem, retraceable to the government outpost of Tiom. We completed this stretch in three days, taking in sights and sounds only the Ndani's could supply. Through open terrain we passed startled natives, saying "Nyak" to the men, lithe, greased, plumed, and empty-handed, and "Laok" to the women, slumped under cords of firewood, mouths stained blood red from betel nut, bark-thread bag harboring either an infant or dozens of sweet potatoes, swinging to and fro, a dire metronome of their tired dance. Gardens extended from river line to lofty ridges miles above, each plot neatly parceled and forever slaved over by wizened mothers of six, hunched over, constantly chopping the cobalt soil with crude trowels. Under vine bridges shiny-skinned youths swam cold swift rapids for sport, while lanky bystanders skimmed wafer rocks from one bank to the other. We jogged along four-inch trails carved into 45-degree slopes – up, and down, and up – stopping to munch molten spuds and steaming greens, cooling them down with crystal water from thin bamboo tubes offered us by pert-breasted, ebony-skinned lasses looking so fine in their reed dresses before their certain descent into childbearing and raw labor. Rain came and went with double and triple rainbows arching across rumbling skies. Back on Justinus' native turf, a gardener spotted him. A hoot followed, then another, and another, until the whole valley thundered with mirthful yelps, hundreds of voices volleying from the water to gardens in the sky.

The administration at Tiom proved thin: one military man (armed), two policemen (unarmed), and a government official, his wife, and seven kids. We had no permission to visit Tiom, but this requirement was waived for a pack of clove cigarettes, with the ensuing conversation saying we could go wherever we choose to. We were led quickly to the home of the Indonesian official (who had never seen an American tourist) and soon we were eating bucketfuls of rice and fanning our mouths from the torrid sambal sauce. Two days later a Mission Aviation Fellowship bush plane landed on the grass airstrip. Seventy bucks later we were in Wamena, where we caught the daily flight back to Jayapura and its repugnant form of "civilization."

It took some local currency and several dollars to get permission to cross the volatile Irian Jaya-Papau New Guinea border, but the dollar always wins in Indonesia, and we soon found ourselves flying for Vanimo and phase two of our expedition.

Bikpela Hol

by Dwight Brooks and John Long

DWIGHT: THE THORNY BUSINESS OF entering Papua New Guinea from Irian Jaya involves leaving a police state – where the Colonial administration's main activity is contending with the daring guerrillas of the OPM freedom fighters – and entering an independent nation, booming and upbeat. PNG welcomes visitors, has ethnological and topographical diversity surpassing Irian's, and places few, if any restrictions on those keen to explore the wilds. Many have done just that. The twentieth century has crept in nearly everywhere, largely due to extremely questionable missionary activity, but a few pockets remain, so isolated that no outsider has yet climbed up or down into them. The problem is to find out where these pockets are.

While kicking around a bottle shop in Goaribari, we met and befriended a formidable individual, vacationing with a steel axe in his belt. Describing himself as an "Assistant to the Sub-Assistant District Commissioner," he pre-accommodated us with a wide-ranging sub-elucidation of why the Enga Province was the most barbaric, least-developed in Papua New Guinea. Following this conversation, we ran out into the street, hopped a Public Motor Vehicle and hung on for two days, hell-bent for a census post called Birip, in South West Enga.

We spilled into the little bush village only to learn that the provincial government had been suspended due to its failure to control the constant tribal fighting. A disgusted Tasmanian anthropologist told us there were no "first contacts" left in Enga, everyone there having been chased from a battle scene by the police chopper at least once. True, there was a certain allure to the plan of photographing Enganese against a ubiquitous backdrop of arrow showers, but we hung on to our initial goal of seeking out unexplored areas.

We did take the time to insinuate ourselves into the Official Satellite Record Bureau of the Suspended Provincial Government. Alone in the office, we read through volumes of patrol reports, apprising ourselves of the current situation, and devouring the exploits of forgotten explorers. The name, T. Sorari, came up again and again, this officer chronicling an unforgettable spate of hair-raising escapades. Assigned to routine village tours, Sorari repeatedly contrived farfetched pretenses for heading off his designated patrol routes into what was then (late 60s) unpenetrated bush. We daubed our brows, packed our mouths, and excitedly agreed that this guy was the real thing.

We were unpleasantly rousted then by one angry Mr. Clementine Warulugabibi, informed by his secretary, Ululiana – whose breasts resembled ripe Wau pumpkins – that "two pela in de" had been rifling government files for more than three hours. He ordered us out, stiffly, threatening to "rifle and shoot" us. John suddenly whirled, and with unusual fervor in his voice, asked, "But, who is this man, Sorari?" Twenty Enganese gathered at the shouting of that name.

"Sorari?" Mr. Warulugabibi barked, astonished, ejecting his quid of betel. "How would two breadloaves like you know about . . . ." He paused, a stern, somnolent expression stealing over his face. "I take it," he resumed with studied gravity, "that you rubbercoconuts have been looking at Sorari's reports. I could calaboose you both. How would you like to sweat it out in the hot-box and eat sago for a month?"

"We ate sago and less for nine weeks in the Strickland Gorge, wantok," John growled intemperately.

I had a Biami sago pounder inlaid with fine slivers of human bone which I produced and invited Mr. Warulugabibi to examine. I hoped this might quell the tension. It didn't.

"Oh, so you think you're a couple of real bush kanakas, do

you?" Mr. Warulugabibi jabbed with an ominous, punishing rise in tone, while flipping the pounder in his hand.

"Hey, John. Steady," I said. All along, the number of steel axes in the immediate vicinity had been swelling.

"You might say that, " John replied. "Besides, those bare feet of yours look plenty soft to me. Where you been lately?"

"John, shut up," I barked.

"No place you'd stay alive very long." Mr. Warulugabibi roared, then suddenly cut himself off, pausing a moment to consider something.

"Mi no laikim go long calaboose," I courteously declaimed to Mr. Warulugabibi, taking advantage of the pause. I'd spent a night in the swamp jail at Daru the previous year, and had no interest in sampling a highland facility.

Mr. Warulugabibi grinned and laughed malevolently. "A service to Papua New Guinea, yes, yes. I've changed my mind. You'll find him in the Gulf Province: our Siberia. That is where the board who drafted his thirtieth reprimand sent him. A patrol post called Kaintiba. Of course, to get in there you may have to face Kukukuku along the way. You'll need more luck than I can wish you, but," he looked thoughtfully at the blackening sky, "I am not going to wish you any luck!"

The door slammed. We knew about the Kukukuku. Once the most feared tribe in the highlands, they are still treated very cautiously by the government, and isolated, uncontacted groups of them are rumored to inhabit nearly inaccessible nether regions of the Gulf Province.

It took some doing, but we made our way up to Kaintiba from the malarial coastal village of Moveave, swallowing gooey sago and sidestepping puk-puks (crocs) along the route. We saw no one.

Kaintiba gained, we made for the village men's house, inside which were stacked some thirty-seven cases of South Pacific Lager, the pride and joy of the District Commissioner, Tsigayaptwektago Sorari. Initially surprised at our arrival, he soon welcomed us emphatically, inviting us in to inspect the hang, and in particular, its trove. The vestibule was guarded by a Sergeant Wanyagikilili, who brandished an M-1 rifle of Second World War vintage. While in no way inclined to refuse the ninth bottle offered him, purchased by us from his stock, Sorari proved himself an astute, witty, and fascinating conversationalist. He sized us up quickly and began talking about various patrols he had made in the surrounding bush. Although cutting a deceptive pose, grinning wildly, constantly-traveling bottle in hand, he had turned an attentive ear to the enthusiasm escalating in our voices the further out his narratives led us. After several minutes we were grilling the man for a unique destination. He suspended all frivolity, composed himself, and made us an offer we could not refuse.

"First of all, boys, no guarantee. You may go a very long way hunting down what may be only rumor. But, I'll tell you, I think there's something to this. For many years, stories have trickled back here about a cave called the Kukuwa Wantaim Kapa Ston, a very gigantic cave; very, very gigantic: truly a bikpela hol."

"Ya-Wa! Nogat! Nogat!" shouted Sergeant Wanyagikilili with fervent dismay. "Duk-Duk, i stap de! Em i got wanpela bikpela *sinek* em i gat sixpela het, fipela tail, em i tausen foot long. Nogat! Me no laikim lukim! Mi nogat tok! Mi go long haus bilong me!" With this, he thrust the rifle in to Sorari's hands and bailed.

I dropped a kina coin into the skull-bank and withdrew another bottle for our friend as John exclaimed, "Man! What was that all about?"

Sorari laughed, pried the cap off with his teeth, handed John the rifle, and took a long pull. "Well, that's the problem. The local people are afraid of the cave, the bikpela hol, and not one of my officers will patrol out to determine whether or not it even exists. Supposedly, it lies ten days walking from the nearest habitation, and that place, about seven days from here, is not a village, only what we call a liklik ples. Most everyone there has died from malaria and sorcery." Sorari shrugged, smiling inscrutably. "Now, Sergeant Wanyagikilili said there is a ghost in the cave, and a snake. The snake is a thousand feet long, with six heads and five tails. He said he is going home because he and this talk about the cave cannot sleep in the same village. His home is twelve miles from here. I am a fairly civilized man, but I do not know what to think. I would like to go, but I can't get away. They'd catch me absent, and I'd be sacked. I'm chained to the radio nowadays, relaying messages from out-stations to Moresby."

The next morning Sorari drew up papers making us temporary Government Patrol Officers (which he had no authority to do) and provided us with a guide willing to lead us as far as Hapayatamanga, the last Kukukuku village before the liklik ples, but not one barefoot step further. In Hapayatamanga, we were to seek out Irtsj, who was under government employ and who would lead us on to the liklik ples, Imanakini. "Irtsj is a sort of a good-for-nothing," Sorari casually added. "He won't want to lift a finger, and you have my orders to be as firm with him as you feel is necessary." From Imanakini we would have to rely on an elusive individual called Ofafakoos, who lived with four wives and many children, some of whom, it was said, had recently been killed and eaten on a payback raid.

We stomped out of Kaintiba on a muddy track that snaked wildly along the contours of a luxuriant ravine. Soon, we were trudging up and down wearisome inclines choked with skin-slashing vines and seething with primordial leeches. Walking on newly fallen dipterocarps was fine. Those recently fallen, still hard though shorn of bark, were slick nightmares indeed. Trees long fallen usually looked recently fallen, which meant we had as good a chance of enacting cartoon cartwheels as we had of plunging into rotted, pungent trunks to our knees, and mingling with the translucent larvae of rhinocerous beetles, discreetly squirming in the friable wood. Mazes of steep rivulets ran everywhere, and were soothing to climb or descend in. Orchids, lianas, moss, were everywhere, large flying things constantly startled us, and our evasive dives were monitored by intelligent lizards. We slogged up to Hapayamaka after only five days.

The enthusiastic reception the machine-gun-speaking Kuku-kukus gave us was encouraging. That good-for-nothing Irtsj, a gangly beast with a walking stick on his shoulder, earnestly translated as much talk as we cared to hear, but he flatly refused to march on to Imanakini: a dangerous place, he said, where the people were controlled by vicious bush spirits who made them harm each other. But, Sorari had sent orders for him to lead us! "Samting Nating!" He did not care. But we had hiked two hundred hours to get there! He laughed. We had trade goods with which to pay him. He said he was sure we would leave Hapayatamanga without them, and laughed again. We didn't, and only after John had threatened his very life did he agree to roust a couple of bolder village boys to lead us off.

Nippongo and Timbunke, perhaps fifteen and seventeen, had just returned from a forty-day cruise in the Western Province, appafently all the way to the Irian border, and, well, maybe a little further, since the ragged clothing they returned with bore labels reading "Dibuat di Jawa" (made in Java) They did backflips when their fathers cut them loose again so soon. They didn't want money, just buai (betel), tobacco, and any excuse to get right out into the bush again. These guys were unbelievably industrious. They'd lead, chattering and laughing, firing back at us exotic fruits and sweet nuts we wouldn't have found if our lives had depended on it. They built rafts in minutes for the gear, then swam the rivers, never just once, but four or five times each. Of course, they'd also have to run half a mile up the bank to ride the river down, and all this only after they'd speared a string of barramundi and whipped up an impromptu barbecue. Rice? They'd rip the bark off a certain tree, fold it into a sturdy trough, build a fire and boil it up. The trough never caught fire. Their bushcraft was ingenious, and we began to see there really wasn't any limit to how resourceful one could be. They were having so much fun maxing themselves they got euphoric. The going was treacherous, no doubt about it, but Nippongo and Timbunke completely transformed our way of looking at the jungle.

During the last twenty minutes before the liklik ples irregular snaps and rustlings convinced us we were being shadowed, paralleled, actually, by men with stealthy gaits. John was tense as a pit viper. Anyone watching the execution strokes of his bush knife could plainly see it. We paused a moment together and strained our ears: nothing. John made it clear he had little interest in establishing a listening post, and blasted off anxiety by screaming up the last incline like a cruise missile. Toward the end I couldn't match the clip, so I brought up the rear in wide-eyed spirals, figuring I'd run straight at anyone making a hostile move and nail him.

Then we hit Imanakini: all two huts, two men, thirteen wives, and nineteen kids of it. They were jittery, freaked by us we thought, but soon guessed not when no one had relaxed a whit an hour after our arrival, and every kid old enough to run was kept prowling on the perimeter. Whoever they were, we never saw them. That they might have been a group of Kukukuku devolving on the hovel for a raid, only to be spooked-off by the odd double white sight was eminently plausible. Fatigue supplanted anxiety later on, however, and we took turns sacking out beneath a teetering lean-to on a bed of fronds, food for every fly, mosquito, ant, mantis, beetle, scorpion, spider and kissing stabber in the whole territory. One old, bedizened fellow, betel eyes out in the Crab Nebula, sat up all night chanting protective spells and exercising his horrendous hacking cough. Another, his toothless mouth a bloodbin, was so paralyzed by fear he never suffered himself to move, save for the spasmodic demands of his frame. The women, naturally, did all the work. We swapped watches, slapping bugs, eventually giving up, hosting all arthropods, desperate by turns to doze. As the night wore on we convinced each other no one was out there, each of us fully aware that in the Asmat, headhunting raids usually took place right before dawn. Then we both went flat. Worse, however, than falling victim to any skullhunt was putting up with the infuriating jibberish of a cock pecking tediously six feet behind our heads. Once home, I would buy a rooster for the sheer pleasure of shooting it.

We slipped out of Imanakini before dawn, following Nippongo along an inobvious brawl of rotting trunks that gave passage through hectares of flora deep enough to swallow a man whole. Eventually we arrived at the bush hut (haus bilong bus) of Ofafakoos, the bitter-end habitation. Queried about Kukukuku raiders, he acknowledged they did sweep through there from time to time, but usually harmed people only when fruit trees they considered their own had pieces missing. Upon being offered one kina per day to lead on to the cave, purportedly eight days away, Ofafakoos grinned extravagantly, thick lips framing a mighty red orifice and two rows of black teeth. He said betelnut offerings tied to certain trees would assure the Kukukuku of our good intentions. He snatched up his bow, six types of arrows, his bush knife and bilum bag of buai, chatted with each of his four wives in turn, glanced askance at John's hand ferreting out a few of the stimulant bulbs for the white man's consumption, then took off through the dripping saw-blades like a track athlete. The unrelenting flurry of machete slashes plied against the untracked jungle by this superb bushman filled us both with enthusiasm and admiration, and distracted us from the starchy, spiceless, boiled gunk of forest tubers we'd gagged down at Imanakini.

Six days followed, during which we traveled in great arcs and weaves, typically climbing a gooey wall adrip with flesh- blistering poisons, needle-like vines, and invidious foot-snaring creepers. We'd top out on choked razorbacks, rest the duration of a smoke, then improvise descents down walls where pitching off meant a 100-foot fall. The only white men who had ever been within fifty miles of these locales were the bold Aussie patrolers who slogged around from Kerema, Kikori, and Malalaua during the sixties.

Ofafakoos would lead a knee- or waist-deep wade for an hour or so, only to step out with spooky acuity and start up another hideous wall. We were truly amazed by his sense of direction. Fathom it? Nogat! Wall, ridge, wall, river: over and over and over.

Understandably, we both began to wonder if he did indeed know where we were going, other than into unfrequented reaches, laced with odoriferous bogs and impenetrable clumps of pink lotuses, fourteen inches across. Day six gave us a view of a forbidding limestone escarpment, a sign which rejoiced us, hinting as it did at cave territory. Next day, after scaling a mud wall on which ice tools and crampons would have been sumptuous aids, I looked at where Ofafakoos had elected to descend. Two Urama Taboo Goblins, ten feet high, their bamboo, human hair, spiderweb, rattan, human bone, sennit, hornbill-headed, pig-tusked, red and gray spiral-beaded eyes frankly terrifying, were staked out as an explicit warning not to continue.

"Dispela olgat det longtim," Ofafakoos remarked uneasily, then spun around convulsively at what proved to be only the loud, chugging huff-huff of a hornbill. Apparently, the people who made these effigies were all dead now, having succumbed to the raids of the uncontacted Kukukuku. With an upward flick of his blade he severed the fibrous weave linking the eerie totems and bolted through.

JOHN: We hurtle down, legs moving like bee's wings so momentum can't tumble us too quickly into the thigh-deep creek, a thousand feet below. After plodding two hours in this creek, under triple canopy, Ofafakoos zags left into a Paleozoic thicket. We're here: a limestone wall rises a hundred yards above. We skirt the wall, then collapse at a clearing. Ofafakoos points to a tiny black hole. The entrance? Hardly the Gothic job we'd expected. Native eyes peer in for sineks while Nippongo, bush knife thunking into a sixty footer, showers us with wedges of meaty wood. Timber! He trots to the high bough, plucking just the right leaf with which to scroll his black tobacco.

"Nogat," says Timbunke: too green. Nippongo shrugs and lays into a hundred footer, felling it only after a pumping ordeal. "Nogat," says Ofafakoos: too dry. Running sweat, Nippongo smirks, then goes for a mammoth hardwood, stopping only when I toss him a pack of Djarums, ferried with much devotion from the Indonesian pirate port of Ujung Pandang. We all howl. Nippongo pings a pebble off my head, once it's turned. We can't wait. D.B. and Ofafakoos dive in as the others stare, jaws agape, making mention of the thousand-foot sinek. "Nogat!" presently echoes from within. Let's go. Nippongo and Timbunke queue behind me.

Within a few feet we find a stupendous tunnel, where manifold veins shoot off into velvet nothingness. Thousands upon thousands of bats are startled into wayward flight. And the hues: ochre walls, stripes of red and orange, swirling dikes of Pan-Ethiopian ivory. Down, down we go, through crawlways into vast, dripping arenas where fang-like columns, seemingly half-melted, loom enormously. The Papuans are forever on guard for the bikpela sinek or its traces. Onward, squirming past clusters of golden stalagmites, crawling through odorous guano under a two-foot ceiling, treading through, then around, the vicious quickmud. We long-jump over bottomless clefts, hooking into warehouse-sized antechambers and dead-end vestibules. I pause at a clean pool, pointing and pining wistfully. Confused, Nippongo trains his gaze, just long enough for me to boot him in.

We've been inside six hours, wandered two, maybe three miles. Though the way has meandered, sporting many aberrations, all now explored, we have invariably returned to the principal shaft. The tunnel ahead looks uniform, extending so beyond eye-shot, but in two hundred feet it starts shrinking, the corrugated floor angling down at a ten-degree rake. The bats are gone, likewise the guano, so our little passage is hospital clean. Bubbling potholes appear – little carbonated springs – with the overflow racing down the incline into pitch darkness. Water drips from the seamless roof. It is probably pouring outside; and while a squall could trigger an interior flood, we figure this cave is too vast to cause a problem. As Nippongo rolls a smoke, we others wash off layers of mud and assorted cave debris from sweat-soaked bodies. It's humid down here! We've left eight-hour candles at strategic bends, about forty so far, but now everything is dank, if not soaked, so we simply advance, the rays of our flashlights swallowed fifty feet beyond. The shaft now angles down sharply, maybe fifteen degrees. Worse, the ceiling is only eight feet above with but ten feet separating the walls. After one hundred yards the water is knee-deep, with wall fissures belching blades of clear juice into our dwindling passage. Suddenly, Nippongo steps into a pothole and disappears. Ofafakoos shrieks: "Bikpela sinek em i kai-kai (eat) liklik Nippongo!" Nippongo pops back up, undaunted, and pointing further down the tunnel, he laughs: "Yumi go now." He's game, all right.

In fifty feet we're chest-deep, and in twice that we're treading water, walls six feet apart, ceiling three feet above. Not far beyond, the ceiling curves down to the waterline. "That's it," I carp. "Dead-end . . . ." Then, from the gully of a truly sick mind, D.B. suggests we proceed – underwater. "We'll swim for it."

"Swim for what?" I beg. Nippongo and Ofafakoos voice doubts in spurts of incomprehensible tok ples (place talk = dialect), bouffants flush to the ceiling, mouths taking in water. A novel sight, all these bobbing heads.

"I ain't going, D.B. We got no line and no idea where the thing heads, if it leads anywhere. Plus once you're under, you can't see jack-shit!" With this, D.B. draws a deep breath and slips into the black. "Damn!" my voice echoes down the tunnel. D.B. re-emerges in five seconds, wild-eyed and rambling.

"Man, is that spooky! We'll have to work it out, five feet at a time. Just draw your hand along the wall so you don't lose direction." I guess that means it's my turn. Nippongo earnestly shouts that the tube is the gullet of the thousand-foot sinek, then laughs. Glug, glug, and into obsidian, just free floating in liquid space. When my stomach turns to stone, I reverse. Wow! I don't know about this. Soon the familiarity of repetition allows more serious efforts, but no results save a solid dose of terror.

We have now ventured out a dozen times each. The shaft has run straight, simple to reverse so long as we return with ample air. But nothing's happening. Need another approach. Yes, forget feeling the wall: put in a few big strokes.

"Okay, I'm going out ten seconds, taking two big strokes, and coming back." One stroke out, gliding directionless through this ink, and I freak, clawing for the wall, then groping back to the fellows.

"That's it, that's my threshold. I'm finished, and that's final." Ten minutes later and we've both gone in twice more, taking three stokes each. Still, we're only staying under about twenty seconds, max. I decide to push it – a little, anyway.

"All right, I'm going for four strokes." Ten seconds, one stroke, two strokes, three, gliding blindly, untethered in space. My arms dovetail forward and pull hard for this last thrust, arms to sides, knifing further into . . . . Bonk! A stalagmite! Hands wrap my ringing head, and for several seconds consciousness and unconsciousness merge. Hands grasp for the stalagmite, which is nowhere, then for the wall, which I find. But what now? The situation overwhelms me: I don't know which way is up, or which way is back. With seconds of air left, my body (not me) strokes out right, my shocked mind but a spectator. Wait! Left hand feels odd, different, and my head raises instinctively to head level: an air pocket, black and soundless.

I break down, gasping, hyperventilating, rubbing my dazed head, nearly crying. It occurs to me that death would be a reprieve. But I won't die unless I stay here. Act, fool! My teeth gnash, my voice is a drone. As the air grows stale, I snap back: find the stalagmite! This pocket is surely past the stalagmite, so finding it anew will point me in the right direction. A sound plan, but even brief exits from the pocket are terrifying. Finally I find the stalagmite, fifteen feet away. Back to the pocket. After a minute of big breaths, I glide out, slither past the stalagmite, hand dragging the wall – but I soon panic and commence with end- all strokes. Arms shoot out and heave back, then out again; but with this pull, I hit something, something moving. It's alive! The sinek! Some massive freshwater eel! Terror magnifies beyond comprehension, and I'm rigid, ready to suck water. Instead, D.B. drags me twenty feet to the thick air.

The light is heaven attained, but my nerves are shot and not until grappling to a dry porch and gasping for minutes is communication possible. Terrified, Nippongo thumbs a thin trickle of blood from my forehead, then rolls me a smoke – which I zip in four draws. D.B. reasons that since the air pocket is so close to the stalagmite, he'll go have a look. I'm too whipped to argue. The five minutes waiting are the longest in my life, but when D.B. bursts back, his face is awestruck.

"It's there! It's true! No myth!" Ofafakoos's eyes pop, thinking D.B.'s found the sinek. "The shaft ends just a few seconds past the air pocket – inside the bikpela hol! There's a river the size of the Mamberambo flowing through the bottom of it. You gotta check it out!"

When in five minutes I'm preparing to do precisely that, a little voice tells me I have a memory problem. Without hesitation, D.B. swims back under. Ofafakoos and Nippongo will retrace the shaft – right now – as the water level is rising. Am I really going back under? Finally, my mind goes blank and I dive downstream, too frightened to stop at the pocket, popping up with a swift revivifying lunge to the flash of D.B.'s Nikon, feeling like I've just been born.

Strange, we're clearly inside, yet there's natural light. We scramble from the pool up onto solid ground. The bikpela hol! Its initial impact is on a par with the Grand Canyon or El Capitan. It takes many looks to fathom the size, later calculated at eleven million cubic feet. We've been treated to the rarest find – a natural wonder of the first magnitude. The river entered through a 400-foot rainbow arch, flowed through a half mile of open cave, then exited through a 200-foot arch. From there, the versicolored ceiling soared to an ultimate apex of eight hundred feet above the water. A one-hundred-foot maw slashed the roof at centerpoint, rife with flying foxes maintaining a clockwise circuit between the dark ends of this massive gash. The swim had gained us a balcony of sorts, three hundred yards long and extending at a gentle angle one hundred yards ahead, ending sharply at a suicidal plunge straight into the river, slow and wide, hundreds of feet below. Light flooded through the colossal entrance and exit, taking us back to when the earth was fantastically new. Unfortunately, at the balcony's far margin, D.B. discovers a tree-line tunnel exiting to the original limestone buttress, one mile downhill from our entry point.

"Too bad," I declaim. "Everyone should have the pleasure of swimming in."

After a hour's gawking (and trundling boulders into the river), we exit into a downpour for a forty-five-minute trek back to the entrance. After two nervous hours, Nippongo and Ofafakoos emerge, well-battered, with horror stories on their faces. Constant rain had made for treacherous flooding, and twice they'd fallen victim to its rage. I quickly dressed wounds more painful than serious, then we charged for a bivouac in the bikpela hol, vast and dry. En route, we marveled over how the terrain could mask our perception of both the cave and its river.

Later, supine and exhausted, I told Nippongo if he didn't rustle up some food, he'd soon find himself diving into the river. He said if I could find so much as a seed pod, he'd give me his widowed sister and her four daughters.

The starved march back to Hapayatamanga thrashed us into hallucinations and slurred speech. The final hours were hateful uphill battles, our only aid the knowledge that we'd stashed four tins of Torrid Strait mackerel in the hut of a Hapayatamanga sorcerer. One tin lay conspicuously open: Nippongo's sister told us that some of the men had been dipping their arrow tips into the uneaten fish. The other three went down faster than we could wince.

The Gulf Province averages twenty-plus feet of rain a year, and I swear we got half that in the following days. Bivouacs were sleepless disasters and food was naught. After seven days, we finally plowed into Kaintiba, and I literally dropped, not rising for twenty hours. We later snagged a lift on a Pilatus Porter from a Kiwi mate bound for Lae, a coastal haven, and spent the next four days at a ritzy expat yacht club, eating and drinking and drinking and eating.

Phoenix: Trial by Fire

How WE FOUND OURSELVES at Norfolk Island is less interesting than Norfolk itself. The native islanders, direct descendents of Bounty muntineers, fled Pitcairn Island around 1856. Thus, Norfolk is peppered with Bounty lore, some of it pretty suspect, like the dark customs crook whose name tag read: F. Christian. It was hotter than Hades, and the next plane was three days off. There was no attraction save the lawn bowling greens behind "Bligh's Bountiful," a worked-up greasy spoon we dubbed "Bligh's Blight." Lawn bowling is boring, so we took to rifling the little balls down the sod, howling when the pins exploded at the far end. We hadn't rolled three frames before the greensman showed. Mack was a fragile, fortyish Australian, whippit thin and nervous as a death adder. Too meek to scold us, he just demonstrated the correct form – a genteel little roll. Noting a Phoenix bird tattoo peeping from beneath his shirt sleeve, I asked about it. He yanked down his sleeve and went dumb. Rudely, I pressed him. He tried shucking us off, which only added to the intrigue.

"You're not really interested," Mack said.

"The hell we're not," D.B. bellowed.

He put out a bit of "young and drunk" stuff, but we weren't buying that, sensing a rare whopper lay behind that phoenix tattoo. Warily, Mack agreed to meet up at the restaurant at 8 pm. A little later, a gardener came over and told us to go easy on

Mack, "since he's a little touched."

That night, Mack started slow and unsteady, but a couple of rums got him rolling. Over the next three hours he squeezed his memory for every detail. He did this not to remember, but to forget. He took relief in writing down various impossible place names, handing them to me as one would hand off a bomb, like he was finally ditching some huge and secret load. Here is Mack's story.

•

After the foiled coup, we couldn't get diesel fuel for the generator, so our only light came from those kerosene lamps that always belch out black smoke; and without fans, the air was brutal. I remember the familiar little messenger stirring in the threshold, like a figure cut from black velvet. When he leaned in with the note, I saw his tears. Bart snatched the message and looked up, shocked.

"We've got to clear out – Sukarno's finished." The little boy moaned something in Bahasa, and my heart sank. Bart replied in sorry tones, and I dug up a couple of thousand-Rupiah notes and handed them to the boy, who backpedaled down the notched log. I'll never forget his big wet eyes, sinking to floor level, pausing, then disappearing. No more thousand-Rupiah notes, no more helicopter rides, and certainly no more medicine.

"They killed his father," Bart started, "because some bastard caught him selling jack fruit to the rebels. We've got to clear out!"

We were mad having stayed that long, but Indonesia held me in its dark magic, and had for five years. I'd made their language my own, and a few of their women as well. Bart had been there seven years, could speak Bahasa like a native, and was essentially Indonesian but for the white skin – and now that was the difference between life and torture. The walls had been tumbling for months, but the total fall of Sukarno's regime really caught us off guard.

"Until the new president, or general, consolidates power, everyone's his own boss," Bart put in. "The people won't bother us, it's the officials." That struck home. All those outpost cops, checked only by a stopgap voice in Jakarta, if at all.

"Jakarta's in flames . . . ." Bart continued studying the message. Since the slaughter of the six pro-communist generals, the entire Indonesian archipelago had suffered a ghastly purge. Just after finding an insurgent floating bellyup in the bog, all the company people bolted – everybody but Bart and me. Suddenly, we were guests of a deposed regime – us, the last white men in Sumatra.

"The company's offering half the cash value of any gear we can personally return to Australia," Bart said. I laughed at that one. Derricks are not the stuff of suitcases, and anyhow, the airlines had stopped operations the week before, when the last of our group had left.

"We're stuck, Bart." I felt ice in my stomach.

"The hell we are," he snapped, "we've got the Pilatus Porter." That plane had pretty much sat on our little dirt airstrip since a long-sacked executive had requisitioned it three years before I even got there. Bart had once taken me up in the Pilatus and let me fly it. I'd been certified to fly small planes back in Australia, but I'd never gotten my solo rating because it spooked me to fly alone. Bart had praised me on how well I flew the Porter, saying most find it too squirrelly to control. But this was only because Bart was with me; he was fearless. Anyhow, the Pilatus was amazing all right, but not without a place to land. We had had to use the helicopters for everything, and even they were often kept at a hover, since every dry inch was usually stacked with drilling equipment. The last copter had buzzed to Singapore two months before.

"Does it even run?"

"Perfect. I fired it up last week," Bart smiled.

"Okay, we dash for Singapore tomorrow. The Porter has that kind of range, eh?"

"Bugger Singapore," Bart said. "The Porter has triple tanks. We can island hop all the way to Derby and pocket 25,000 G's apiece. The Porter's worth 100,000 as she sits."

That kind of coin had a handsome ring, but the thousand-mile junket to Australia seemed a long shot in a little bush plane.

"You reckon the outer islands won't be as hot as Java?"

"Could be worse; we'll carry our spare fuel aboard and land only at the Mission Aviation Fellowship strips. I figure they're getting leaned on too, so we'll only stop long enough to refuel.

Those MAF strips are in spots where only fool missionaries want to go. We'll sneak by okay. I figure to do the entire two thousand miles in one long day."

"Two thousand miles?" So we wouldn't be flying in a straight line. I put up an argument for Singapore – just a hop – but I knew where that plane was heading. Bart had worked all over Indonesia, and could fly the Pilatus Porter like a pro. I couldn't complain about the pay, anyway.

"We leave at first light. The boy says they're already setting up roadblocks. The police will come looking tomorrow, you know it."

I grabbed a couple flashlights and we made down the footpath to the company strip, so infrequently used that no one would search it for some days, or so I hoped. I doubt the locals even knew what lay beneath the big, green tarp. I set to ferreting out 55-gallon gas drums as Bart, with a flashlight clamped in his teeth, went over the engine. In twenty minutes the Pilatus roared awake, then shut off.

"Everything okay?"

"No, but the plane's fine," Bart sighed.

With the gas drums lashed tight, and the triple tanks brimmed, Bart lay back on a passenger seat resting in the dirt. We both were covered in grease, and the flashlight started flickering just as Bart began plotting on the aviation chart. I volunteered to fetch fresh batteries, but Bart went anyway. I milled around in the dark for a while, but when Bart didn't show after ten minutes, I got nervous and went looking for him. As I struggled along the black footpath, a sound made me hold up about hundred yards from the house. Suddenly, the whole place burst into flames. A dozen people scattered away. Outlined in the glow, they held up in the swamp to view the blaze. Several looked to be holding petrol cans. Their arms waved, and they shrieked with a vengeance. One man had a rifle, or a machine gun, and probably meant to shoot dead anyone who stumbled out. He wasn't just aiming at the flames, I can tell you. When nobody showed, they left, screaming and carrying on. The house was quickly gutted. Then the walls collapsed, the piles gave and the whole place crashed into the swamp with a hiss. I'd never made friends easy, but Bart and I were fast mates from day one, and when I thought he'd been torched in the fire I panicked and started running back to the plane, tripping and groping over the creepers. You can imagine my surprise to find Bart back at the plane, pumping some gas into a greasy pan.

"Follow me."

He sounded real bitter, and it was much later before I realized he felt himself betrayed by people he had known for seven years. We marched the quarter mile to strip's end, where Bart set the pan down.

"I'm jogging back to the plane. When you hear it fire up, wait two minutes, light the gas here, then sprint for the plane." He handed me his lighter and trotted off. I paced around like a lunatic. A hot current welled up in my throat and my ears rang. The notion of striking out into the night seemed like mad fiction, but the Porter's roar told me otherwise. I ripped a pocket off my greasy shirt and waited. My watch showed 3:10 in the morning. As the minute hand crawled past 10, 11, I lost nerve, lit the pocket and dropped it into the pan. Whoosh! The night came alive and I dashed for the plane. With the click of my door, Bart freed the brake and the screaming Pilatus vaulted for the distant flame.

"Come on, baby," Bart screamed, "get up now!" But the Pilatus was overloaded. The flame drew closer, got bigger. Suddenly we burst through. The landing gear dragged through the mangroves and I swear to God we just cleared a hardwood grove further on. Bart set a course for Bapuju on the south coast of Borneo. Frozen into my seat, I peered down but could see only a few lights blinking through dark clouds. We hadn't gone six miles when hailstorms pelted us hard, and in another minute, sharp crosswinds were tossing us all over the sky. Visibility was zero. Bart bent over the stick, trying to follow the twitching instruments. Without headphones, we couldn't even talk over the engine, so when the storm grew so wicked the gas drums started bouncing, Bart pointed his finger straight up, then yanked the stick back with both hands. We finally broke through about 18,500 feet. My teeth were chattering and I was lathered in a glacial sweat. I remember just staring at the moon.

"Can't go around weather . . . . Got go straight or lose bearings . . . never find strip," Bart screamed. I started feeling kind of queasy and must have swooned, because my next sensation was bumping through patchy gray fog. Bart puffed hard on a cigarette and looked pretty confident. The altimeter read 10,300 feet. Before, I hadn't noticed that Bart's forearm tattoos were greased over, and my clothes were shot with gas, grime, and mud. A little green oxygen bottle lay between us, and Bart later told me he had huffed it dry, having gone over 21,000 feet to dodge currents. I checked my watch: 7:30. We found the Bornean coast in twenty minutes, and Bart quickly located the Kahajan River, which we tracked fifty miles inland to the MAF strip. Bart and I had been there three years before. The strip was just a swath of dirt, stuck in a narrow canyon, so once we committed to land, there was no pulling out. Bart circled once, then dove into the cleft and shimmied onto the uphill strip, uphill to compensate for its puny length. Momentum carried us to the dirt's last few feet, and as we taxied around, a man ran toward us from the flanking jungle, screaming: "Don't shut it off, don't shut it off!" Bart set the brake and we got out.

"Who are you?! Why did you land?" the man demanded. "You got to leave, you got to leave right now!" The government had grounded all the MAF Cessnas a month before and the missionary, a tall, thin, Texan, seemed certain our visit would get him and his family killed. I frantically rolled out a gas drum and set to work.

"No!" the missionary yelled, "you've got to leave, you've got to clear out! I beg you to take off right now!"

"We're dead empty!" Bart screamed, waving me to hurry up. "Give us five minutes and we're gone, I promise you!" Drunk with panic, the missionary paced in circles, biting his index finger, looking like he expected rebels to converge on his jungle mission. Instead, his wife came over, carrying a handful of mangoes. He went right at her, ranting and waving his arms. She stood mute, and I was rolling the empty drum into the ditch before she joined us. I smiled, grabbed the mangoes, and hopped aboard. In two minutes we were blasting over treetops fringing the Kahajan River. We arched hard over a gleaming mosque and tracked a beeline along the uniform coast, extending forever, blue and green, leading nowhere. The beach finally fell away, and even now I can picture the lonesome horizon, so swollen with open ocean and blue sky. We were alone, and desperate, but the mangoes tasted like heaven.

Bart's plan, as I understood, was to stop at another MAF strip in south Sulawesi, just north of the capital city, Ugung Pandang, about 280 miles to our southeast. Unlike Borneo, which was little more than tall trees, Sulawesi was a boon of resources, and was essentially administered by Javanese. I heard stories about the people of south Sulawesi, known as the Bugis, and renowned for their dark skin, treachery, and pirateering. Rubbish, I thought, until Bart told me: "Count your lucky stars there's a MAF strip down there!"

The mangos hardly slackened my thirst, and I was real hungry. We'd been airborne about seven hours, hadn't slept for thirty. The harder I stared at the ocean, the more it seemed we weren't moving at all, but were pasted to the sky, the water rushing backward like a blue treadmill. It just went on and on and on . . . .

I woke with a start. My mouth felt pasty and my lips were glued shut. Despite the open windows, the sweltering cabin was rich with fumes and the engine thundered about my head. Bart's free hand rummaged about the first-aid box until he found another ampule of smelling salts. He popped it straight away and waved it under his nose until his eyes gushed. I peeled the last mango. The sun was overhead, and the Sulawesi coast came into view before my head cleared. I took a jolt of smelling salts and the coast was still there. Bart chewed hard on the mango pit, sneaking glances at the chart on his lap. I felt pretty jaded. The engine roared on.

We couldn't find the MAF strip. We had buzzed miles of jungle, every river, canyon, and valley, until the fuel needle quivered just off the E.

"Got to land . . . take chance at airport . . . no choice but to land," Bart screamed, pointing to the fuel gauge. If Bart had a fear threshold, it was somewhere in the stratosphere. I was way over the line. We charged back to the coast where Bart pointed below to a big black gash hewn from the green. Several squat huts and some jeeps lay at the far end, as well as three old transport planes. We didn't have the gas to make a fly-by, so Bart set us down and we taxied to the far reaches of the tarmac.

I jumped out onto rubber legs, but before I had even unlatched the side door the jeeps were on us. Bart leaned in and turned off the engine, but the roar still echoed in my head.

A dark youth in camouflage fatigues had dropped to one knee, submachine gun leveled on the plane. Two others in khakis and berets held a bead on Bart and me. A fourth soldier, with medals pinned on a black waistcloth, cautiously paced over to the plane, his pistol drawn. A dozen eggs hung from the brim of his hat. Bart said something in Bahasa and the officer wheeled, surprised at Bart's fluency. It seemed ridiculous that people were always amazed at our fluency in Bahasa since the language is so simple. The officer looked at the plane, took several steps forward, looked back at Bart, then peered into the hold. Satisfied, he began imploring Bart in guttural Bahasa. The soldier in fatigues took to his feet and led me over to the open jeep. The khaki-clad soldiers, or policemen, leaned on their guns, smoking furiously, enraptured by the hot dialogue between Bart and the officer. The officer couldn't find a suitable voice – he tried several – and his few words were more confused than angry. I felt to vomit from the tension, but Bart remained composed – or he looked it anyway.

They finally poked Bart into the jeep as well, and we drove off toward the huts. The officer barked something, then paced over to an administrative shack; the soldiers rammed us toward a downtrodden shanty that roared with voices. Once inside, a dozen or so astonished soldiers fanned out to surround us, staring, fidgeting with their rifles, smoking hard. The smoke was thick but it couldn't mask the stench of raw sewage. The soldiers began with trenchant quips, but they dummied up when Bart replied in perfect Bahasa. They tried other dialects, but Bart knew them all. Unable to hide behind their own language, they just stared, completely unashamed, like monkeys, and I couldn't have felt more awkward standing on my head. The officer returned and shouted us onto a bench. He barked the soldiers through the door, then he too went outside and started screaming. There was desperation in his voice.

The shanty had no windows, and despite two open doors, the air was stiff with humidity. In the corner, a little Bugis guard, not yet a man, sat behind a desk, smoking and staring. Then through the door came the unmistakable sound of shovels, piercing the ground and flinging their load aside. Several crisp voices got the shovels working doubletime. Several other officer types entered our shack, and after taking our few papers, they variously instructed the young guard. I was very concerned about those shovels, but from my angle I couldn't see anything out the door. Then a rifle shot sounded and the new officer dashed outside to join some arguing voices.

"What the hell's happening?"

"No talking," Bart said.

"What do you mean, no talking?" I begged. The guard pulled a pistol from his belt and tapped it on his desk. Bart's face looked like a baked apple.

The lead officer returned after another rifle shot and a great volley of screaming outside. He looked pleased. He gave the guard a curt order, then went for the door only to get pushed back by a prisoner in chains, urged along by three armed guards. So mud-covered was the prisoner that I couldn't tell his condition, though his step still had some spring despite the leg irons. Whatever, it wouldn't matter for long.

The boom of thunder just outran a curtain of rain that hammered on the tin roof. I presumed the voices had fled, but when the squall passed, the shoveling and arguing quickly resumed. The moisture helped defuse the stench, but the smoke and humidity were fearsome.

Carrying a great bowl of rice, a haggard native passed before us, doubled over to keep her head lower than ours. I noticed her shuffling bare feet were intricately tattooed up to mid-shin. Her ear lobes, loaded with brass rings, were easily six inches long. But for a tattered sarong, she was naked.

"A Teraja native," Bart whispered. "They're treated worse than dogs."

The guard tapped his pistol on the desk and the old native set the rice down there. Several more prisoners entered the hut, likewise prodded by automatic weapons. Barely clothed in filthy rags, they were sweat-soaked, exhausted, and abused. They didn't fancy going through that door, but if they slowed, the soldiers rammed them in the back and they stumbled outside, heads down, condemned men if I'd ever seen them.

Ever collected, Bart traded comments with the Bugis guard. I tried to lose myself by staring at the opposite wall, attempting to pronounce the impossibly long name of a politician whose photo was pinned to the wall. Just to its left was the name "Pak Sukarno," the current president – or autocrat – who this revolution was out to depose. Sukarno's photo was missing, apparently ripped from the wall since white corners were still tacked to the reeds.

The Teraja woman returned with a huge bowl of boiled pig rinds peppered with a sambal. Just as she set it on the desk, a shot sounded and the old native hit the deck, her head so low her ear lobes raked the dirt. The guard dumped the pig fat over the rice, then dropped the empty bowl at the woman's hands.

"Ayre," the guard shouted, pointing outside, then kicking the old maid in the hip.

"Ayre!" She wouldn't move, she wasn't going outside for water, and if the guard was to shoot her, she'd take it right there. But I sensed that punk wasn't up for murder. He kicked her again, harder, rolling her over like a dead animal. Then another shot, followed by fifteen voices yelling over themselves. The guard jumped to his feet, screaming, "Ayre, Ayre!," while viciously beating the hapless native. She wailed. Outraged, I stood up. The guard drew his pistol and waved me to bench it. For a moment I just glared – not from courage, but hatred – then I backed off.

"Ayre, Ayre," the guard resumed, pummeling the native whose wails mingled with the madness outside.

"Ayre, Ayre – " Again I jumped up.

"Stop kicking her, you coward," I screamed. "Stop kicking that old woman." The guard wheeled and I stared straight down the wee barrel of his pistol, his eyes focused behind like two black marbles.

"Sit down," Bart ordered, "you're going to get us both shot!"

"To hell with this whole place and every dog in it." I knew that young guard couldn't shoot. If so, he'd have been outside. Gun shaking, the young guard was too flustered to note the battered native slither off, and instead blew into a tantrum. Ever resourceful, Bart laid out an elaborate excuse, slowly, which vexed the young Bugis, but set him down just the same. I sat down as well, staring at a name I couldn't pronounce, at a face I didn't know.

"You heard me," Bart started. "I said you were a Moslem scholar and demanded to know where the Koran sanctions kicking helpless women. I doubt he believed it, but you better start acting like Allah or we might get shot after all."

"After all, you think they're just going to let us gas up the plane and fly off?"

"They'll have to," said Bart. "But it might take hours. This isn't my first encounter."

But everything said this was our last.

"You've never been in this kind of bind before. Don't tell me otherwise."

"I've been held at gunpoint before," Bart deadpanned.

If shame has a short memory, that guard had amnesia. He tore into the mountain of rice and pig fat, grease streaming from his open mouth. He'd forgotten about the Koran, forgotten that we weren't to talk. Another group of inmates was dragged through the shack, and a soldier seemed to joke with Bart. Bart smiled with his lips, but I knew his gut was churning from more than the fetid stench of sewage and clove cigarettes. At face value, his sham moxie might have settled me, but I wasn't looking to relax with executions going on a hundred feet away. I felt the thump of my heart. My greasy shirt was soaked through. The soldier in jungle fatigues marched in and told the Bugis guard something that set him organizing the shack, though there was nothing to organize. He repositioned the desk in the dirt, nodded to the soldier, who left, and then sat back and started cleaning his fingernails with his fork.

"The big man's coming," said Bart. "We'll get things sorted out."

"Yeah, I bet we will," I cracked. My voice scared me. Bart started talking Bahasa with the guard, who continued cleaning his nails.

"I hate that bastard," I cut in. "They hate us and we're dead because of it."

"They've got no reason to kill us!" Bart snapped.

"Do they need one? Did that sap in rags give them a reason? This whole place is in shambles. We're history . . . ."

"You're crazy," Bart whined.

"They're crazy," I insisted, pointing outside, "and I don't fancy spending my last moments listening to you chat up that Moslem."

"Last moments?" Bart implored. "You want to bet on that?" It took a moment to fathom that bet.

"What do you mean, bet on that? Bet we're going to die?"

"That's right, if you're so damn sure about it." For the first time, Bart looked like I felt. "Put up, or shut up."

"Put up what?" I laughed. The whole thing was so asinine. The Bugis guard was so enchanted by our argument that he stopped digging his nails.

"Put up what, my life?" Sweat ran into my eyes. "My life to win, or if I win, I die?"

"Exactly," Bart chuckled. He was Bart again.

"And if I lose?"

"You get the tattoo of your choice, once you're back home."

Home. He could have said Mars. The bet was ridiculous, but I started turning it over in my mind as a diversion. Bart had always pestered me to get tattooed. He regretted his and just wanted me to affirm my recklessness. But I'd never been reckless, ever. Still, squirming on that bench, I came to like that bet, if only to prove myself wrong. I extended my hand. "You're on, Bart."

A voice approached. The Bugis guard snatched his pistol from his desktop and stuffed it into his belt. He dragged his sleeve across his mouth, then snapped upright in his chair. A little brown man entered. He wore a pressed, short-sleeved suit, was unarmed, had no badge or medals, and moved with distinctive Javanese confidence.

"Ah, yes, the Americans." He spoke English with a thick Dutch accent. He dismissed the guard with an upward flick of the hand.

"Now, gentlemen . . . ." But first he ordered the guard back to remove the disgusting bowl.

"What kind of Moslem eats pork?" he asked in English. "Now, tell me about your unexpected call to Ugung Pandang."

Bart didn't hesitate. "We're heading for Australia and stopped to refuel. I hoped to use the missionary strip but couldn't find it."

"Why would you choose that dangerous missionary strip when you could land here?" asked the official. He had to be an official.

"Yes, of course" he came right back, "because you're flying a private plane, which is illegal in Indonesia. It's subversion, particularly now."

I saw the conclusion to his thinking, or heard it outside.

"Our plane isn't private; it belongs to Reeves Oil, which we've been managing in Sumatra. I've been there seven years, but until the government firms up a little, we've been ordered out. In the process, we stopped here. No choice, mate, we were out of gas. It's all that simple."

"If you've been here seven years, you know nothing's simple in Indonesia," said the official impatiently. Something in his mien indicated we were in big trouble. "Even company planes need clearance and your papers show nothing. I find nothing to connect you to this plane whatsoever. Did you steal it? How do I know you won't fly it into the presidential palace, full of gas?"

"That's preposterous," said Bart. "We're flying away from Jakarta."

"Yes, as you say, that's preposterous . . . impossible. Not because of your direction, but because you white people are never that dedicated to a cause." I sensed he wanted us to divebomb the presidential palace.

The official smiled and walked on over to the door. I had never seen a man look as serious as Bart did just then. My teeth were gnashing hard. "I can't breathe in here, gentlemen. Please join me outside, where we can hopefully find a solution to our problem."

"Let's talk this over a little more," Bart suggested. "We're here at the government's request, for Christ's sake!"

"Your hosts have been deposed," said the official from the threshold." I started pleading, and the official looked confused.

"Gentlemen, please, let us talk outside."

"Let's go," said Bart, matter-of-factly.

It seemed all wrong not to make them drag us outside. When I rose, I thought I might find some honor in going willingly. I didn't. The sound of those shovels was like being whipped.

Outside, the ammonia stench of sewage overwhelmed me. Surprisingly, the officer walked us away, pausing only to yell at some armed soldiers supervising ten shackled natives digging an immense pit. The soldiers had bandanas stretched over their noses and mouths; the filthy natives did not. The officer kept pointing to a photo tacked to a cluster of bamboo stakes shoved into the dirt. The face on the photograph was so pocked with bullet holes you couldn't tell who it had been. The soldiers all played ignorant and simply nodded to the officer's last orders.

"The soldiers are most incorrigible," the officer stated, turning to lead us directly toward the strip. "When they should be working, they take wagers on their marksmanship, firing off their guns like children. The septic tank exploded yesterday, and it's very dangerous if we don't immediately fix it. I've had to pull in convicts, since the soldiers are too lazy to dig – these Bugis are most incorrigible. Now let us walk to this plane."

We marched straight into the sun. My feet felt like lead, and my head was on fire. The officer didn't look around when he talked, and I didn't like his measured speech; something was all wrong.

"The police wanted to shoot you, but you spoke the language as well as them and they didn't know what to make of it. Now, you have a plane that nobody here can fly; otherwise we would keep it. I suspect you have money, but that, too, is no good right now. You have no clearance for Sulawesi. I have many problems right now, impossible problems, so I won't add yours to my list. You'll have to leave immediately and deal with things as they come."

"The timing of all this is no coincidence, is it?" Bart demanded.

The official smiled. "None at all, my friend. And don't land at the missionary strip, or I'll have the place burned down. Good luck, gentlemen. Salamat Pagi." He turned and walked back along the black strip.

"Bastard!" Bart yelled. "You son of a bitch." Still in earshot, the officer didn't look back.

"Shut up, you idiot!" I ordered. Bart's eyes were murdering the official, who was now lost in the shadows.

"It's almost 400 miles of open ocean to the next island, where the only strip is risky at high noon; and there are no lights! It's almost dark, eh? We're fine for takeoff, we'll find the island okay, but we'll never find the goddamn strip. We'd just been handed a death sentence because that cur's too frightened to shoot us."

"He might be, but those others would drill us for a smoke. I'll take my chances with the plane."

"You'll have to," Bart moaned. It was a black moment. Suddenly Bart laughed, spat, and began rolling out a gas drum. "Buckle up, mate, we're going for it!"

Despite my horror, I realized something fantastic was going on. The officer could have bullied, tortured, even shot Bart, but he couldn't have *made* him fly into predictable doom. That kind of boldness – or madness – already had to be in place. The Java boss had spotted the crazy white man right off and knew he would go for it.

After three and a half hours of flat-out, black terror, we saw the moon emerging just as scattered fires on Wetar came into focus. I understood that Wetar was then so superfluous an Indonesian holding that no one would have cared if we'd have set down on the national strip – had there been one. Spotting a few lights on the dark beach, Bart began circling lower and lower. If he had a plan, I didn't know it. This epic had taken the fight right out of me, and I just wanted something to happen. I was sick of discovering how much more I could take.

Bart buzzed in dangerously low, and we could just make out where the surf met the sand. He screamed to hang tight, then he set us down on the wet-packed sand inches from the surf line, with difficulty, since the wheels were bogging and a lunging nose wanted to auger us in. How he saw where to land I'll leave to luck, since a foot either way would have finished us. Bart jumped out, took a quick look, then quickly hopped back aboard.

"No stopping or she'll sink . . . fill her up fast . . . gotta go for it!" How, after fifty hours, could this guy still be yelling: "Hurry up, we're going for it!"

"Let the bird sink, bring on the soldiers; I don't care!" But my body automatically rolled out the sixth and last drum, and I spent thirty minutes chasing Bart with a hose as he jockeyed about, never stopping, the landing gear rowing soupy grooves into the sand. Nobody came from that huddle of lights, four hundred yards away. Maybe they were spooked by the screaming engine, which had driven me mad two islands ago. Covered in gas, I flopped into the warm surf, so much wanting just to melt into Wetar. When I crawled back inside the plane, I prayed the engine would explode. The salt on my lips reminded me how thirsty I was. We were going to Australia, 300 miles due east. It was 10:40, and Bart hadn't slept in days. As we charged back down the beach, I closed my eyes, not that I could see anything with them open. I was convinced this gauntlet would never end.

The surf had revived me, but hallucinations soon rose off the silver ocean: black horses, mountains, icebergs. I even saw the prop whizz off, leaving a flange rod spinning, the engine screaming. Everything was imagined save the truck lights on the highway south of Derby. All I recall is the sensation of a rough landing.

•

"You okay, mate?" I didn't know who I was, nor where I was. A hulking truck driver with sad eyes was looking down at me. After landing, I'd somehow gotten out of the plane and passed out on the ground. We'd put down beside the transcontinental highway, in wide open, barren country. The driver handed me a burlap- covered canteen and I went to drinking like crazy.

"You okay?" the trucker repeated. "Yeah, yeah, I'm okay, but we better get some water to the pilot." The trucker just stood there, looking at me real funny. I stumbled to my feet and went over to the plane. Empty. Bart was gone. I got frantic and started yelling; but you could see twenty miles in every direction so I reckoned Bart had gone for help while I was still out. The trucker was going to Perth, far to the south, and I got a ride with him. I told the trucker about our trip, but I doubt it made good sense because I was still pretty beat.

When I arrived in Perth, the cops hadn't heard anything from Bart, which worried me. When I suggested a search party, they kept stalling, and real soon an executive from Reeves Petroleum showed up. He'd never seen me before and had to check my passport photo before he'd believe I was me. This astonished him. We went into another room, just us two, and I started going over everything. The executive was looking real concerned, and all at once he cut me off.

"We've just learned that rebels burned down Bart's house in Sumatra. We thought you were inside it somewhere. Bart was. I'm sorry."

"That's impossible," I screamed. "The guy just towed me 2,000 miles across Indonesia!"

"That's one hell of a piece of flying, and the reward is all yours," the executive assured me.

"Tell that to Bart when he shows up – and he will," I promised. "You just wait."

But I'm tired of waiting. Real tired . . . .

Meltdown

IT TOOK TWO DAYS to fly to Pangnirtung, near the southern toe of Baffin Island, in the Canadian arctic. It was mid-March, and even the Eskimos – or Inuits – were frozen. My first priority was to scout the mile high west face of Mt. Thor for filming in July – a likely ploy that would allow an arctic snowmobiling trip and plenty of time to take in Baffin's huge rock faces. Rarely seen, these granite monoliths have an almost mythical reputation, and the smattering of published photographs further the mystique.

In Pangnirtung's only lodge I met a stalwart young Inuit named Tommy Kilibuk who agreed to round up two snowmobiles and join me on the recon. He suggested swilling the remaining coffee and heading out straightaway. I hadn't slept in two days. Tommy said he hadn't either. What with the perpetual light, the signal to nod never comes. We pulled on layers of silks and polypropylene, donned huge duvets, wrestled into animal hides, then stumbled out into minus ten degree stillness. Tommy had rounded up the fastest snowmobiles in town – rumbling, 500cc monsters that blasted us out over the vast and frozen fjord.

●

Twenty minutes out we spot the Guardian, with its bold, 2,500-foot profile. With international climbing teams mounting expeditions from the Baltoro to Sarawak, it seems impossible that this plum should remain virgin. Tommy says a French team scaled the lower face, but bailed at the headwall, leaving it for others.

While it is my design to cruise and memorize the scenery, this is hopeless owing to the speed I must maintain to stay with Tommy. The ice is no longer hard packed. It is granular, like a snow cone, which makes for squirrelly going at sixty miles an hour. We enter Auyuittuq National Park, pierce the imaginary boundary of the Arctic Circle, and motor into the melting, sloppy falls – not a proper falls, but a summertime rivulet now a frozen staircase of ten degree ice steps. After three hours we've hauled one 300-pound machine onto flat ice. Exhausted, an ocean of expresso cannot keep us up. We pitch a tent, slide into forty pounds of hides, and die for ten hours.

Tommy bounds into consciousness as if he's spring loaded. We brew up, then start laboring the other machine over the ice step. Tommy's sealskin boots paddle on the ice while my spine bows, desperately absorbing the three hundred pounder. We fire up the machines, then glide toward Thor. Distances deceive. Thor swells, while never drawing closer. The falls five miles back, we achieve the last passage.

Through a roofless ice tunnel, we advance. The passage is gray. As the ice recedes, light floods in and the valley is revealed. The snowfield extends for miles, ever uniform. Out left, a ridge of rugged peaks jags north; to our right, Mt. Thor prevails. Backlit, its 6,000-foot shadow bisects the snowpack at centerpoint. White and black. We pause at the shadow's threshold. The sky is blinding blue. There is no wind, no sound. We motor along the shadow's edge, skids straddling the line of light and darkness, two flawless grooves trailing, one faint, one not. Just left, melting snow glimmers. My right skid grates on the ice. Again we stop. Nothing moves; my ears hum.

We pass the next two days among gray granite walls awesome and fantastically couched. Mt. Thor (or Thor Peak as the topographic map denotes) seems too grand to fathom, its summit looming 5,700 feet above the glacier. We motor north and spend hours leisurely studying the one-of-a-kind Mt. Asgard, whose 3,000-foot east face hosted Rick Sylvester's ski-parachute descent as the opener for the James Bond thriller "For Your Eyes Only." From certain angles Asgard looks like a perfect smokestack – uniform, vertical, with a summit absolutely flat, as if lathed to exactness. How ironic that climbers in Yosemite should for generations rake over the same old cliffs, looking for something new, when nearly everything we see is unclimbed, and Asgard alone has potential enough to exhaust a million ambitions.

The weather holds, so we putt about according to our whims. The magnitude of it all, coupled with the strange stillness, makes us feel like travelers on another planet, alone and amazed. We rarely eat, never stop, and only reluctantly head back when cooled by the second midnight sun. Idle wandering is past when Tommy guns it at the Thor Glacier and we rocket toward the falls. Once there, he slows only to bounce down, crouching, cursing, laughing; then he resumes top speed.

With Tommy bombing in the lead, we power-drift around an outcrop. Here he throws up an alarmed hand, locking up his machine and skating sideways to the juncture of land pack and sea ice. One glance is enough. The fjord's edge is ringed in jumbled, icy blocks, all bobbing in a foot of slush. Glare ice gleams half a mile out, but that too looks bleak inasmuch as it bears an increasing veneer of meltwater. With the rising tide, the whole mass moans and crunches from the ocean's pulse. Forty light-hours have transformed an inflexible courseway into a hideous tract of uncertainty. A basso groaning belches from the ice.

Tommy looks grave, saying that while the fjord's center has ice yards thick, the perimeter, especially during breakup, always has treacherous bubbles. Puncture one and you're into the brine – and dead in minutes. I consider ditching the machine and tromping a ridge forty miles to Pangnirtung. Unnecessary, says Tommy, revving his engine. He says that speed is safety, translating to less time spent on marginal ground. At speeds beyond seventy- five, he claims, one can traverse ice the thickness of eggshells. However, there is one absolute rule: "Never stop, ever." Tommy's eyes focus on that point of safe ice some ways out.

"Remember," Tommy says, "carry great speed . . . full throttle." Then, like a thunderbolt, he fires off.

My eyes wander up the surrounding peaks, vaguely shaped, indistinct. The sun is overhead; no shadows. Now, well past the park's startling geography and miles shy of the Guardian, there's nothing arresting enough to lose myself in, to forget, if only momentarily, what lies ahead. But there . . . a solitary bird.

Tommy is just a shrinking dot on the white. Again my eyes join the lone bird, lofting up a buttress. Then, ZIP! With my head still sideways, birdwatching, my right hand has dialed the throttle up to full bore. A throaty two-stroke shatters the arctic calm – a white rooster tail explodes behind, the belt chews in, and the 500cc's vault me onto no-man's-land. The chunky surface means an eighty-five horsepower bull ride and it's a wrestler's task to hang on. Accelerating, the rig slips, slides, and crashes over floating blocks. As the surface levels, it thins drastically. Meltwater settles in low spots, giving the illusion that the ice is paper thin. Fifty miles per hour is achieved; only moments have passed before firm ground is a mile behind. Thirty-nine to go. The surface is still bumpy, but as I hit eighty miles per hour, I enter a half-mile stretch smooth as an ice rink. Instantly the machine is skating – sideways and unsteerable. The belt whines on the ice with no effect. Now backwards, at seventy, skimming like a hockey puck. I enter a mottled section. The belt digs in and the effect is like dropping the clutch: the engine dies without a sputter.

As I slide to a full stop, frightful sounds pop off the ice. As last momentum ebbs, the belt carves an ever-deepening rut which fills with water. And that chilling sound, like snapping glass, continues on and on until my perimeter is crack-laced. I start yanking on the starter cord. "Come on, sucker!" Thin wafers of ice start tilting in. I'm sinking. Every combination of throttle and choke brings no result. My chest heaves. On my toes to keep the water from pouring in my boots, I think the rope will snap if I pull any harder, or faster. For a second, I'm studying myself from afar, from the summit of that frigid peak – this frightened kid is on nowhere's edge, yanking on a cord connected to a sinking machine on a great mass of floating ice. He is scared, panicked, and pulls still harder on the cord. But nothing happens.

Just audible over my whining comes Tommy's sloshing trot. That he should return amazes me. Winded and soaked, he wastes no words, just flips up the engine housing and cups a gloveless hand over the carburator. "Pull!" he gasps. With the first yank, the ice groans and we sink another four inches. I yank again. The engine hacks – it's flooded. Through gaping fissures belch the tide's basso notes, silenced only by intermittent water springing forth. "Again!" The engine coughs, farts, then revs to a shrill din. Good thing, because I've just yanked the starter cord off the sprocket. Water and ice shoot from the speeding belt. Everything's soaked. Our feet churn in deep slush and my hands are numb from heaving on the cord. I would have ditched it long minutes ago, but now we've sunk so deep we need the machine's velocity to pull us out. In a forty-foot circle, the ice has sagged, like a coin on loose sheets. To plunge through is curtains. Despite a feathered throttle, the machine gnaws deep into the ice. The ocean groans, then leaps forth, a plume of water spraying behind. We've chewed through! Backsliding, the nose comes up and it seems certain we're all going in. Now tilted forty-five degrees, the belt catches on the hole's edge and wobbles forward. Under quarter throttle, the machine claws up over fractured plates, dragging us out of the slush, only to backslide, then lurch forward. A last backslide and we finally gain level ice. Feet dragging, I'm clutching the seat strap as Tommy fights the bars. Maintaining about twenty miles per hour, we both leap onto the seat and immediately enter another ice rink. As Tommy's machine nears, he goes side-saddle. Then he jumps off at speed, sliding for fifty feet on his sealskin boots. Like some stunt wrangler, he jack-knives up onto his machine, left running, but half sunk.

He applies full throttle and we're now side by side, at fifty, sixty miles per hour, racing over the same kind of surface that had nearly finished us minutes back. The ice is crusted and glassy. With every patch of glass, with every cough of the screaming engine, with every drift of the skids, I age a lifetime. Then the crux: at eighty miles per hour we rocket onto a five-mile stretch of wafer-thin trash. Water flows beneath the bubbled surface. After half a mile, we've ground eighteen inches into the fluted skin. Oddly, we can maintain the shocking speed with the trailing rut affording some stability. I can't tell if we are chewing further into this trash and it's a torturous guessing game as to where that last layer is. A quarter inch below? This seems the logical place for that bubble, but I can't consider these thoughts because I'm desperately hanging on at eighty. Slush flies everywhere, but we carry on.

The worries are for naught when in a mile we sail onto solid ice, the thrill of our thin escape fueling us well beyond. Only slowly do I realize our new and equally serious jam. I'm panting and my torso is frozen. Soaked and on a snowmobile at speed, little time elapses before one becomes stone cold. We are covered in so many layers of wool and hides that it is not so much frostbite as irreversible hypothermia that threatens. My hands are wooden, so steering involves draping an equally wooden arm over the handlebar and pulling with my shoulder. My machine is ploughing a drunken course and each bump jolts out more warmth. My legs are senseless from midthigh down; my stomach is knotted, my face is cast in cement. I'm getting kind of woozy. With the lodge in view, we both lapse into chilled stupors. Left on its own, my machine putts around in a drunken circle, then freezes to a stop. Tommy is hunched over, speechless. Neither of us can crimp the throttle. We're mere sticks in the snow; without immediate aid, we're finshed. The rest is a dream. Spotted by some kids, we are raced to the lodge where the girls take over. I'm hurriedly stripped and taken to a tub of tepid water. I have no feeling anywhere; my eyes roll and an unimpeachable drowse is arrested only by the slapping, screaming girls, who won't let me nod. As they try to bend my limbs, I'm force-fed hot liquids. This all happens in ultra slow motion. Minutes flow together. Everything begins to recede, but life comes back with my first sensation, a remote titillation that grows into a writhing, electric jabbing, like ten thousand hat pins punishing my flesh. As nerves come alive, I am tortured back to here and now. Water churns from the tub as they rub and manipulate my agonizing body. When my eyes clear, I'm amazed to find a girl – fully clothed and waist deep in the tub – sitting on my chest and rubbing oils on my face. She smiles and looks so confident I relax. Whack! She slaps me back awake. When the pain eases to a hot glow, they carry me to the polar bear rug and start kneading my flesh, palming blood into ever-warming limbs. Dreamless sleep.

•

Tommy kicked me in the ribs, told me to put some clothes on. Several girls were still massaging me. One, whose gorgeous round face could fill a hula-hoop, told me I'd been out for several hours and had talked all kinds of shit. I felt a little worked, but otherwise okay – not a mark. Slipping into some trunks, I slouched back onto the polar bear rug, eyeballing the mounted narwhal tusks, the intricate soapstone carvings, the century-old harpoons. There was little to convince me I wasn't the luckiest man in another world.

Star Wars Comes to Wabag

DWIGHT BROOKS AND I were kicking around Mt. Hagan in the Highlands of Papau New Guinea, licking wounds after an exploratory thrash down the Strickland Gorge. That's five weeks of rice, and more rice, so we presently gorged on jungle pastries, washing them down with South Pacific Lager. After two days, we were jumpy for another epic. Our flight to Sydney would leave in eight days, so it would have to be a quick one. A notorious rock star and charlatan had just helicoptered in, stopping for the night before heading for a guided tour of the upper Sepik. The rocker had told us his plans several months back, and we had written them off as party babble. Our surprise was less than his, and he offered us a lift to wild Telefomani. Seeing his entourage of gusseyed-up Hollywood waifs, we passed. (We later learned that the waifs turned back at the first mosquito. The rocker, however, carried on like Lord Jim, spending thirty days in primal bush.) That left us only to read the newspaper before heading back to the bakery. We were bored.

D.B. burst out laughing, pointing to a blurb headlined with "Two Die in Enga Fight." I read the story: "Two men died of axe and arrow wounds on Wednesday after a fight broke out between Lyonai and Kundu clans outside of Wabag, in Enga Province. Joseph Yalya, 38, of Pina Village, died of an axe wound to the neck and Tumai Tupige, 39, also of Pina Village, died from an arrow through the chest. Police said about 800 men were involved in the fight. The fight broke out when Lyonai tribesmen accused the Kundu clan of using sorcery to kill a Kundu elder, ..."

This sounded like a suitable place to spend a few days, so we packed and caught a ride from Barry, an Aussie ex-pat who was driving to a reservoir project at road's end, 30-odd miles past Wabag. For several hours Barry described the huge tribal wars that still rage today – wars that yield to passing cars and sometimes break for lunch. There are plenty of histrionics in this "warfare," as evidenced by only two deaths in the reported 800-man brawl. Like the other fights we'd seen in P.N.G. (and unlike the "do or die" affairs in Irian Jaya), they resemble some crude form of rugby, minus the ball. Still, when we pulled into that shithole known as Wabag we were disappointed not to continually duck a salvo of arrows and spears. Rather, the same old routine: Kanakas (bushmen) dressed only in ass-grass (Kunai grass shorts secured with a rattan belt), with axes over their shoulders, feathers or boar tusks through septums, and jowls full of betel nuts and disgusting, blood-red spit.

Now Saturday, Barry suggested stopping at the bar, then sauntering over to the theater, where "Star Wars" was playing. A bar? A theatre? in *Wabag?!* They don't even have a store! Barry claimed "Star Wars" had played every Saturday night for two years.

We checked into the Wabag Lodge, an open-air dive with running bath (river), then made for "the bar." No Roxie, this was a cage of double chain link, the cashier and the stock of beer inside. You pay first, then the beers are slid through a tiny slot in the chain link. I won't go into the long-range dart games, or the other diversions going on in the forest around the bar. We hammered down a couple of beers, then made for the theater.

To our great misfortune, the movie house was not an open air job, but a converted cement garage used previously to store the province's three tractors. A boisterous queue of Kanakas passed slowly through the tiny entrance. Exclusively dressed in ass-grass, they were obliged to check in axes and hatchets, receiving a number to reclaim them. Several were confused by this procedure but were quickly pacified by a gigantic black official, easily six feet, six inches tall. Inside, 150 people jammed like cordwood into the little bunker. Several benches were in place, but most Kanakas chose to squat in the oily dirt. The front wall was whitewashed. The ancient projector sat askew on a bamboo table. The heat was oppressive, but the aroma could have wilted a brass bouquet. The Enganese diet is almost entirely forest tubers and manifold shrubbery, and they continally pass a crippling wind, unabashed, and most sonorously. Combine that with knee-buckling body odor, the fetid stench of betel nut expectoration, then box it all in a ventless cement bunker, and you have the Wabag theater.

The gigantic official barked in pidgin, and the crowd quieted. He flipped on the projector, which ground and clanked. He compensated by cranking the volume *way* up, which distorted the dialogue beyond anything human, but made the sound effects interstellar wonders. As a 50th-century spacecraft burst into a trillion pieces, terrible moans issued from the mob, and more than one Kanaka took to the dirt beneath the benches. During the scene when Han Solo wrestled the Whatever, a row broke out in the corner. Just as it looked to escalate into a riot, a torpedo-busted mother of six squealing kids swung her bilium bag of spuds upside a Kanaka's head, and all eyes returned to the wall. Later, a dumbstruck Kanaka stole up to the wall to "feel" the projected images. He turned around, squinting into the light, and was soon bombarded by sweet potatoes and betel-nut husks. He screamed, the crowd howled, the giant barked, and the bushman bolted back to his bench.

The end credits rolled out and the wall went blank. A short silence was followed by demands for more. The giant projection-ist/manager/official yelled "no gat" (no got more), but the mob was not inclined to believe him, so to avoid a certain riot, he simply rolled the film back in reverse. A trillion flaming particles miraculously coalesced into an intact starship and flew off with a woosh! Great cheers boomed from the crowd. More farting, more yelling, more spitting . . . .

King of the Jungle

TAKE ANY SUPER-REMOTE OUTPOST and you will find a full complement of loners, touchy scientists, and sociopaths. They gravitate to such posts; plus, most veterans will admit, anyone spending more than a year "out there" is never quite right afterward. Whoever can remain unshakably sane becomes the uncrowned king in such outposts. He may be a cook, a missionary, or a crooked prospector, but he is king just the same. Such was Plutarco Campos, who I had first met at an outpost in Venezuela's Territoria Amazonas, a horrific tract of malarial bogs and rain forests bordering Brazil. Pilot Miguel dos Santos introduced us. My "mucho gusto" sounded casual, but I couldn't stop staring at Plutarco as he loaded the helicopter. A dead ringer for Simon Bolivar, I quickly realized his smile sustained everyone living in that wretched place. His bare feet were more calloused than a Kalahari bushman's and his tattered dungarees, shorn at midshin, were secured with a twine belt. A Herculean torso indicated he was one of a few non-Indians to do a lot of raw labor. Plutarco was ever shadowed by his dog – a colossal mongrel missing an ear who looked about ten pounds lighter than the helicopter, and twice as strong; and the copter was a three-million-dollar Sikorsky that could haul a dozen men, Plutarco's dog, and an entire communication system in its hold.

The engineer finished topping the tanks and flashed a thumbs up. "Two minutes," said dos Santos. The compound boss, an odious 21-year-old named Suárez, suddenly rushed over to Plutarco and started ranting. If Plutarco couldn't find the destination, Suárez would cuff him; and God forbid Plutarco didn't finish his work in two days because the generator still needed fixing before Plutarco went to another distant place on Wednesday, and the general was coming on Saturday, and he too wanted a word with Plutarco, plus something had been stolen from the radio room and Plutarco would have to sort that out too, and, ay caramba, what the devil did Plutarco think he was doing standing around when there was so much to do?

I had briefly met with Suárez an hour earlier. I was in the Amazonas shooting jungle vistas for a new King Kong movie (which got yanked from the theatres before I could even see my work) and the film commission in Caracas promised me some flying hours in the chopper. Not so, said Suárez. They had too much work and too little gas to charter it just then. But seeing that the chopper went far and wide every day, I could tag along and film. Fair enough. But still, I cared little for Suárez, who seemed a bitter punk with a boulder on his shoulder – and his tirade just proved it.

Plutarco's hound jumped in back with me and Plutarco's young Indian assistant, and in one minute we were arcing over the tall trees. Studying a chart in the co-pilot's seat, Plutarco checked off certain rivers and mountains he could make out through the mist. Crisscrossing shafts of amber light burned through holes in the clouds to glint off great meandering rivers. If any place bore the aspect of an alien planet, it was 4,000 feet below. Dos Santos nabbed the chart, leaving Plutarco at the helm – which I likened to handing the space shuttle over to Huck Finn. Plutarco's bare feet deftly worked the pedals, and he had a soft touch with the stick. Though hardly a licensed pilot, he had spent thousands of hours aboard and could fly well enough for dos Santos to study maps and instruments, or even grab some shuteye. Eventually we found our destination, a tiny clearing on a vine- choked mountaintop. As we shimmied down, Plutarco hopped out to guide dos Santos onto a mottled limestone slab, the blades whizzing close as your next breath to the surrounding jungle.

The young Indian assistant bounded out, shouldered an over-and-under shotgun, and began a revolving vigil. "Snakes and big cats around here," explained dos Santos. As the hound scoured for both, Plutarco unloaded chain saws, axes, machetes, gas cans, and his meager bivouac kit. Construction on a micro-wave relay station would begin once Plutarco had cleared the area. Fat chance. An atomic bomb might clear space enough for a totem pole. As I set up my camera, I envisioned Suárez's rancor after Plutarco failed at his impossible chore.

Boom! A shotgun blast. I wheeled to see the mutt plunge into the hedge to return with a very dead bushmaster. The Indian reloaded. Plutarco revved his chainsaw, smiled, then laid into the jungle like a man possessed. To watch this was to watch a man head-butt a bank vault.

The mist increased to a light shower, nixing any filming. Dos Santos wanted to leave before we got weathered in, and as we coptered off, he pointed to the headphones, wanting to talk.

"I know what you're thinking," dos Santos chuckled, "but you're wrong. Plutarco can do anything." There's something wonderful about a person who feels he can do anything, but that only makes failure doubly tragic.

"He can try," I put in.

"That job's routine for Plutarco." I smiled. Dos Santos explained. As a young man, Plutarco had fought over a woman from Anaco. He did not start it, and it was not known if he killed his man or not. He did go to jail, however, where he worked forced labor clearing jungle for future highways. There, dumbfounded prison guards beheld a veritable Pablo Bunyon, who, they claimed, did the work of fifty men – and liked it. When first-world technology came to Venezuela for good, communication sites had to be erected in the meanest jungle. Initially, the army was to clear these sites, but scores were maimed by tigers, snakes, and stupid accidents. Enter Plutarco. At first, he was assigned to a crew of militia, who only watched him work. In time, the whole task was handed over to Plutarco, his Indian sentry, and the awesome hound. Over the years, the authorities had not so much dropped, as forgotten, Plutarco's sentence. But Suárez would remind the entire compound of it hourly.

Suárez met us at the heliport, as livid as ever. First, that imbecile Plutarco had taken the wrong shotgun shells, not the ones Suárez had flown in special, and Suárez knew the half- wit Indian would fire on every insect, so they would run out quickly, and should a tiger show, Plutarco would die – if there was any justice in the world – but then the laggard would never finish his work, nor could he talk any sense into that Philistine general on Saturday; and Suárez kept on like this all the way to the mess hall.

Suárez punted a sleeping dog in the threshold, and we stepped over several others to join ten men with sad eyes, chain smoking and discussing when Plutarco would return.

"Not soon enough," Suárez cut in. First, there was the office thief, and what was Plutarco going to do about that? Furthermore, outside tending a stricken dog was an Indian who had to see Plutarco about his sick daughter and, hijo de puta, Plutarco would ford the Orinoco in flood to help an Indian but the ass couldn't even fix the generator. If Plutarco hadn't cleared a hectare by tomorrow, Suárez would see that Plutarco spent the rest of his life punching out license plates in the Cumono Penitentiary. He kept rambling about Plutarco until dos Santos and I fled to his quarters.

The sloth of outpost life can drive men to the hardest liquors, especially when sharp rain pins you inside. As dos Santos struggled to tune an old guitar, I took a shot at the Gideon, but threw it aside.

"What gives with Suárez, anyhow," I wondered.

"God hates Suárez," said dos Santos – and he explained.

Suárez married at 18, and to support his wife and infant child, he took a job far beyond his experience: the catch was that he was sequestered in this remote compound. In his absence, his daughter died and his wife took another man. The wife's father – a local political boss – had his attorney annul the marriage, and for his trouble the lawyer made Suárez sign over the newly purchased house, the car, everything, to the ex-wife. Suárez felt his wife still loved him, and he knew her father had authored the whole scenario. But if Suárez was ever seen again in Estado Carabobo he'd be shot dead. In one cruel sweep Suárez suffered more grief than a boy of 18 has a right to know, and it struck his naked heart like a cannonball. Suárez fled back to the compound a full-blown blackguard – and had progressively gotten worse.

Late the next day I whirled off with dos Santos to fetch Plutarco. We had trouble finding the right mountaintop, which I did not even recognize when we finally did. The once-meager clearing now looked like Iwo Jima after the invasion. In an area the size of a baseball diamond not a blade of grass now grew. The dog looked dead, the Indian half dead, and Plutarco slightly less, though haggard – not from the brutal labor, but because of the jaguar that prowled their camp last night and which, without shotgun shells, they staved off only with the roar of chain saws and the howling of the tethered mutt. When the gas ran out at dawn, things were touch and go as Plutarco finished off his work with only a machete and a hand saw. Two minutes aloft, the Indian and the hound were fast asleep.

Back in the compound, Plutarco hoped to just eat and pass out, but Suárez demanded he first pass judgment on the office thief. If Plutarco refused, Suárez would break out the shells that Plutarco forgot. Plutarco had not forgotten the shells. He had taken the right box, but some fool had switched shells. For a long moment Plutarco stared hard at Suárez, who went off even worse. Ten minutes into his meal, Plutarco was ordered out, to go set up court.

Fifteen Indians, dos Santos, and I followed Plutarco to his house, a scrap-metal shanty with a dirt floor. Several tiger skins hung on the walls, along with a cracked mirror bearing a faded photo of Plutarco with a striking Latina. A small chest lay in one corner, flanked by a cot facing benches for twenty. An Indian lit several hanging lamps, and soon there wasn't room enough to change your mind. Then Suárez entered, dragging an eight-year-old wailing Indian boy who bit and wrenched free to go death-grip Plutarco's leg and gush out words only Plutarco and the somber Indians could make out. Suárez swore hard, rubbing teeth marks on his arm. An hour's heated exchange revealed the boy's crimes: As he swept out the radio room, someone had mistakenly locked him inside. During his five hours therein, the boy found a box of chocolate bars and ate them all. Suárez suggested a week at the trowel. Plutarco said an hour of sweeping would do. They went back and forth, Suárez growing ever angrier until he slammed his fist on the bench, demanding draconian measures for the boy's "crime." Ultimately, Plutarco decided a half hour on the rake would do. "And that's final," he added. Suárez, his jugular vein looking like a crimped hose, ordered everyone out, then he scolded Plutarco for twenty minutes. Through the open door I saw Suárez draw his face close to Plutarco's: "I hate you, Plutarco."

"I know you do," Plutarco smiled.

"That's one miserable man," said dos Santos, "and he's barely old enough to drink!" Of course, Suárez was more than miserable, he was psychotic; but I still could not figure his ceaseless hatred of Plutarco. After Suárez stormed off, we joined Plutarco on the hour's march to the Indian's village. The natives received Plutarco warmly and led him straight to the shack of the sick girl. She had recovered somewhat but still could not walk. "Dysentéria," said Plutarco, after a thirty-second check of body parts and a few hushed words. I don't know what else Plutarco said, since it was all in the Indian tongue. The adults nodded slowly, with keen understanding. A little later, a stooped old woman came in with fried plantains and other fruit.

At daybreak the next morning we all coptered off to another far- away plateau, finding after fifty minutes a puny clearing with three radar disks. Plutarco and company bounded out to wage battle; dos Santos and I chugged off in search of the perfect camera angle. Shortly we found a primal vista of swollen rivers and green cliffs, and after only an hour I had more than King Kong deserved. Plutarco had reckoned six hours for his task (a week for Rommel's troops), so dos Santos and I caught three hours of sleep while Plutarco fought it out two valleys away.

Back with Plutarco, I was not surprised to see that the clearing now resembled a Zen sand lot. Flying back, Plutarco said he would skip dinner and just go collapse. Ten minutes from the pad we hit torrential rains and just managed to wobble in as the storm grew worse. Braving the downpour in only gym trunks, an anxious Indian told Plutarco that the little girl had relapsed. Plutarco dashed off, and returned in a pounding squall, cradling the girl, now wrapped in blankets and a plastic tarp. Constant vomiting had dehydrated her to a mere wisp of what I'd seen only the previous night. The electrician, who doubled as the medic, took her temperature: 104. "Cholera," said Plutarco. The little girl was delirious. Plutarco tried every combination of soups and teas, but she could keep none of these down. She would die without IV's, which we didn't have; the nearest were in Falcone, forty helicopter miles away. "It's suicide to try and fly right now," dos Santos put in between great peals of thunder.

"But we can't just watch her die," Plutarco grumbled, arguing that the flight was worth even the greatest risk.

"I'd try it if it was simply risky," dos Santos snapped, "but I can't even lift off in this storm." Indeed, an absolute hurricane pounded the tin roof, howled beneath the building, and looked to drown Suárez, who was chased through the door by such gusts it took two lunging men to shut it. "How is she?"

"Critical."

"That's impossible!" Suárez insisted. "She just relapsed!"

"Look for yourself," Plutarco said. But Suárez would not, or could not face the young Indian's demise, which grew more certain with each minute. I was surprised with Suárez's pacing, which roughly translated to disgruntled concern. "Do something, you fool!" he screamed at Plutarco. But nothing could be done. Hunched over her daughter, the Indian mother moaned so miserably that it drove Suárez and dos Santos into the radio room to see if and when the storm might pass.

Curled on a small candlelit cot, the little girl was quickly withering away. Plutarco mopped her scalding brow and tried to squeeze water from a towel into her mouth – with no success. Now chilled, now burning up, her ebony limbs were enfolding onto her torso, into a shriveled fetal form. Coma could not be far off. It was the purest hell watching the little thing die while we just sat around impotently. Hopelessness finally drove me to make the thirty-yard survival march through shin-deep streams and jet black driving rains to the radio room. I found dos Santos yelling into the microphone and straining to hear replies that were patchy at best. The transmissions came from a terrified operator at an outpost forty miles east. The storm had already swept away one of their structures and was threatening the operator's very office. He was signing off and bolting for higher ground.

"Coward!" Suárez screamed.

"They've got their own emergency," dos Santos said. Other

tries at communication were hopeless. Suárez screamed into the storm as he left. It was now 2 a.m., we could only retire and hope the little girl hung on until the storm blew over. It gave no sign of doing so as we sprinted for the aid station and Plutarco. The situation was the same, but Plutarco had left, probably forced out by the woman's plaintive moans and his utter helplessness to assist.

"Plutarco will come back," the woman cried in hack Spanish. "Plutarco will come back and save my niña." I hoped he wouldn't, hoped he would save himself the grief.

The storm checked my sleep to a light doze, and I tossed awake at first light. Outside, save for a light mist, the storm had passed, so I stumbled over to a vexing scene at the aid station. Plutarco's giant hound stood guard and would not let Suárez enter, nor would anyone inside answer. One step too close and the dog would growl, showing his teeth. Decoys were helpless. Still no answer from inside. I trotted off to Plutarco's house, but found it empty. Back again, I found dos Santos begging Suárez to put the gun down.

"Answer me or I'll shoot the perro, I swear it!" Suárez wailed. But no reply came from inside. Suddenly Suárez raised the shotgun and dos Santos jumped before it – a foolish move just then.

"Señor Suárez, señor Suárez," cried a running boy from afar. "Señor Suárez, the helicopter. It's gone!" We dashed for the heliport, and after rounding a bluff in a quarter mile, we staggered to a stop, staring ahead at an empty cement slab. Suárez was shocked beyond words.

"He must have left during the storm," dos Santos began, "else we would have heard the bird fire up. There are only three places he could have tried for . . . ."

"I'll kill him!" Suárez screamed as we strode for the radio room.

We first tried the closest outpost, forty miles east. They were frantic trying to sort things out from a brutal night: they had lost two of their eleven structures. And no, no sign of any helicopter. "Are you mad?" the operator begged, after dos Santos laid out the truth. Suárez was strangly mute throughout, slumped over the other radio, waiting for Plutarco to call in. It took another two hours to hail the next outpost, fifty miles south. The operator had seen nothing of any helicopter, but he described in a high whine how the storm had punished his compound. Our prospects were looking poorer by the minute. In thirty minutes the third and last possible compound called us. The storm had decimated the outpost, and they requested assistance. Six were injured when the roof collapsed on the commissary, and they were presently without victuals.

I argued that there must be other destinations that Plutarco could have shot for, but with the gas he had, dos Santos assured me, there were none. How about a search party? With what? We had – or once had – the only copter in the whole region. And even if we could search, we were ringed by a million square miles of jungle that could swallow a squadron of B-52s and never show it. Add to this the sad fact that we hadn't a clue, not one bearing to commence a search, and we might as well search for a lost coin on a Waikiki beach. If Plutarco had a live radio, he would certainly have contacted us by now.

"It's over," moaned Suárez. As he moped off, I saw someone who had no desire to live another minute. Of course, he hadn't hated Plutarco at all, and in his desperate attempts to reach out to another man, he found he could only lash out: his black past would allow nothing else. A boundless despair spread through the compound. I saw grown men cry like infants, and the sight of Plutarco's dog still guarding the aid station cut to the quick. I felt like some demonic author had penciled me into this black fairy tale.

As if God himself wanted to bury the hatchet, the general soon called up. Learning that the storm had passed, he would chopper in at late afternoon, and please have quarters ready should he choose to spend the night. This, of course, depended on how his conversations went with Plutarco – and their meetings were legendary. I never did find out how the general figured into the compound, but it fell to dos Santos to inform Suárez of the situation. He dragged me along to buffer the nightmare. We found Suárez in his office, head down on his desk, lights off. Dos Santos stuttered out the news, and Suárez replied in a quavering whisper.

"Yes, I'll explain to the general, and he can take me to the penitentiary." It almost seemed that Suárez wished this on himself. "And I didn't switch shotgun shells on him. I couldn't have done that to Plutarco. I just couldn't have." So we just stood there, benumbed, saying nothing. Suárez was so overcome he could never see that Plutarco's self esteem was the outcome of his dueling the impossible. Without that contest, Plutarco was a peunrious stray with a dull machete and no salvation, and he couldn't live on that. So he'd struck off into a typhoon, and the odds had caught him. But there was no consolation in any of this, and time was frozen in that humid little room.

In an hour that could have been a year, a frantic radio operator burst into the room: "He's on the radio, he's on the radio . . . Plutarco's on the radio!" Suárez exploded from his chair, overran his desk, and stampeded over dos Santos in a mad flight for the radio room. After about three steps, a cord from a small floor heater entangled his ankle. It caused him no pause, and the heater bounded behind him, first smacking dos Santos upside the head, then bouncing behind Suárez for another dozen strides. Dazed, dos Santos dusted a boot print off his chest, and we rushed to join a gathering crowd at the radio room. Suárez ripped the phones off the head of the beaming radio op.

"Plutarco?"

"Si, señor."

"How are you? *Where* are you?"

"In Brazil, Jefe."

"Brazil?"

"Si, Brazil."

Plutarco had beelined for a huge mining compound, eighty miles due east. He realized that, in the horrendous storm, he couldn't find the other company outposts, but knew he could find the Brazilian outpost by following the valleys he knew so well. The girl was responding nicely to IV's, but she could not be moved for two, possibly three, days.

"Three days?" Suárez laughed. "I'll be lynched by then. The general is coming in three hours!" It was quickly agreed Plutarco would bolt for the compound posthaste, and that dos Santos would fetch the girl when she recovered. Dos Santos and Plutarco exchanged some technical info, then all repaired to the helipad. In an hour the crowd had swelled to over fifty Indians and every hand in the compound. The first popping of the distant chopper caused uncontainable excitement, and as Plutarco feathered down onto the little cement X several folks had to be physically restrained. As the king was reunited with his people, emotion got the better of many. Plutarco said the flight wasn't so bad after all. Plutarco and Suárez exchanged some rare banter, and dos Santos whispered that it was the first time he had seen Suárez smiling in two years. Swiftly seeing that seventy-five people were staring, or rather smiling at him, Suárez went dumb, quickly scanned the exuberant crowd, and wiped the watermelon smile off his face. He grabbed Plutarco and shoved him toward the compound. "The general's coming, you imbecile, and just look at you – like some bleeping pirate smelling like a week-old carp." And Suárez could have Plutarco shot for stealing the helicopter, which he might recommend to that fool general, though Suárez was still undecided about that. But either way, Plutarco would first repair the generator if it took Suárez's bullwhip to see the job through. And just like that, things were back to normal, though despite their best efforts, neither Suárez nor Plutarco could erase the tight grins completely off their faces.

Auyan Tepui:
A Fool's Pursuit

THE JUNGLE! That first sight overwhelms, hypnotizes, shatters my concept of the wilds. What appears a vast green carpet is actually a towering thicket of treetops, upwards of 100 feet. Tortured by equitorial rains and swelter, the constant green fans out past infinity; the mightiest forest would vanish in it's shade. It is said that a murderer sees red before he strikes. God must have seen green before He spat on the Venezuelan rain forest. So spurned, the flora rioted over the land, and great trees burst through that ripe undergrowth to produce their own hideous miracle. Clouds dash above the treetops in a constant flux of renewal. Below, oblivious to all but its own pulse, each thing gropes skyward as if every limb vied for the same shaft of light. The organic surge is absolute. The odd photon trickling through exposes the mangled jungle floor, dark and impassible. Troops of monkeys and flocks of pastel parrots glide on top, and you wonder if even they know what is ten stories below. Anything entrapped serves only as so much mulch for the next generation, restlessly forthcoming.

•

Bridwell's call came at four in the morning.

"Get packed, we're going rappelling. Leave in two days. Oh, and bring your passport." Click . . . .

Surely this is a rude gag, a whim call from some debauched party. I try and reinstate my dream. Tossing, turning. The problem is: while many of our mutual efforts have ended as laughers, Jim Bridwell isn't one to jest. Worse, his offhand plans, usually drawn in passing, usually mean a debacle in the offing. Worse still, I can never refuse.

A few hours later, still prone but no better rested, I get a call from a producer at David Frost Productions, who apologizes for the early call while commending me for taking the job on such short notice. It seems Jim has volunteered me to "procure the necessary equipment to break the world's record." The producer will wire me the money for all necessary purchases. A record, you say? She laughs. I soon learn we are to break the continuous rappel record by descending Venezuela's 3,300-foot Angel Falls. A batallion of cameramen will capture the event for national television, leaving us to shoot the close-ups with a "wee Bolex." Don't know, lady. Sounds sort of bogus. But after she quotes a fantastic fee, I'm on the phone to Royal Robbins, placing an order for the longest damn rope he can get us.

The following days are a blur of collecting two-way radios, a visa, typhoid shots, etc. Only with the aid of friends do I gain the airport fully equipped, though exhausted. Snagging the Red Eye out of Las Vegas, I hook up with Bridwell in Miami, where we hop a Varig flight and drink ourselves to Caracas.

A lazy sun swells off the gray horizon as we pile into a salt-pocked cab, massive coils of rope and alpine crap draped over, around, and under our every limb. Once loaded, the cab's body nearly hits bottom, with the cabby exclaiming that his fee will consequently double. "Fee?" laughs Bridwell. "Who cares? ABC's paying; step on it, hombre!" As all expenses are covered, we have no hankering to scrimp, and will go on to blow money extravagently. This is to the chagrin of Danny, an unctuous, swarthy, porcine twit who has just joined us, and who will slash and cuss at us until that day when we are all scared beyond words. His harping is just the standard trash of a producer trying to flex authority, and we pay him little heed. But he's such an unrelenting scoundrel that it becomes our practice to goad and gall him whenever possible. Tonight, hoping to further rile him, Bridwell pores over the wine list, and not knowing Grand Cru from Red Mountain, Jim simply opts for the costliest bottle. Danny explodes. We chuckle. He will never convince us production money means anything to him, and it seems a half-assed show of power to question our expenses. What's a three-hundred-dollar bottle of wine?

Once settled, we make for the production house that will supply our film gear and also Roberto, a jovial, alabaster-skinned Italo-Argentinian now living in Maracaibo. A rush-hour drive through central Caracas is a spectacle of motorcycles engaged in mad slalom. The scenery admits the incredible rift in class structure. Flanking the hundred-story, marble Xerox building are scores of grimy shacks plying chicharones and volcanic coffee, while Latinos, Negros, and all admixtures mill about, some New York clad, others in rags. Hillside shanties, the houses of Chilean and Columbian aliens, distend from the crumbling dirt cliffs way out onto bowing forty-foot piles. Pounded by rain, these homes sometimes crash and burn, notes the cabby; then they just wash away. Traffic is stop and go but the cyclists still zip in and out at speed. Horns sound, the humidity rolls, curses break the thick air. A hearse pulls alongside, its gleaming black carriage sagging under unknown cargo. Bridwell figures that dozens of dismembered cyclists are in there, "stacked like cordwood." I tell Danny he'll be joining them if he doesn't quit hounding the cabby for greater speed.

"Hey, shut your damn trap!" snaps Danny. "You fools just worry about the falls, nothing else."

"Amigos," asks the cabby, in Spanish, "what's with the asshole?" Bridwell and I trade knowing looks. In time, Danny will get his due, we'll see to that.

Three miles and two hours later, we arrive at Roberto's film studio, Roberto forever translating dry jokes into fractured English as Bridwell and I try to get a handle on camera gear so ancient neither of us knows how to load the magazine. Roberto has been hired as a coordinating producer, and the ten people in his three room office are hustling over final details. Bridwell and I steal eyefulls of the secretaries, svelte and curious – "no habla English" – but who cares? "Easy, boys," laughs Roberto, "that's my wife." "But does she have any friends?" begs Danny. And that's the end of that, the secretaries not given to his fat leer, his bossy demeanor, his lacquered hair.

Finally all things are squared away, leaving us to face Roberto, who presently asks if we know why the burro crossed the road. Antsy, Jim and I are dying to roam Caracas as we're charged with the volts of new and foreign turf. Also, we need an hour without Danny. It is into the jungle tomorrow.

The next day we board a battered DC-3 heading for Canaima, the little settlement tucked into the jungle some forty helicopter minutes from Salto Angel (Angel Falls). No phones, no hot water, and I can only wonder how the production team – now twenty strong and accustomed to luxury – will settle in. Shooting is still ten days off and there's surely little to do in Canaima, save jungling around or drinking.

As the DC-3 grinds up into the clouds, the ocean melts into stark green jungle flowing with slow brown rivers. In thirty minutes the terrain grows precipitous; innumerable waterfalls fire off rocky mesas and striking, vegetated cliffs. Now we're rim high with what Jim calls an overgrown Yosemite. Look at that . . . a stupendous limestone pillar whose summit is three times the girth of its foundation. All passengers are marveling except Danny, who demands another scotch and looks a little pale. "Nice flight, eh, Danny?" He snaps, apparently terrified of flying. We've got him now, I think.

The pilot's cabin has no door, and my inquiry of the bronze-skinned stewardess says I can intrude at will, which I do. Meanwhile, Jim's face is flush with the glass, eyeing this wonderland, astonished. The pilot, whose smile hosts a cigarette, cannot be older than twenty-five. He steers with one hand, the other a blur of gestures accompanying surprisingly good English. There is no co-pilot, so I grab that seat. Introducing himself as Pepe, he urges me to take the helm. No problema. Bridwell shows and panics when Pepe (the pilot) feigns sleep. Laughs past, we explain our intentions, hoping for a fly-by of the falls.

"Ay caramba!" cracks Pepe. "You want adventure, I give you adventure." He must enjoy a thrill, for there are no roads, no radar, no nothing in Canaima; that leaves him only these valleys for a guide, and they're usually hammered by torrential rains. Smiling slyly, Pepe promises a bird's eye view of the falls, but he too has a request. Will I watch the ship for a moment while he goes to the head? Relinquishing the controls, he rises and is immediately shoved back down by a panicked Bridwell: "No way, babe!"

"Jaime! How disappointing. I thought you like adventure." Then Pepe cracked that crafty smile of twinkling, golden teeth. Dead reckoning, we wail on at rim level through the Auyan-Tepui (Devil's Mountain) valley, its dripping walls ever widening, steepening. The western mesa, off which tumbles Angel Falls, reaches an ultimate height of 8,200 feet.

Often cloud-shrouded, this prehistoric landscape lent the original impetus for Arthur Conan Doyle's "Lost World," and one half expects to spot a Tyrannosaurus Rex snapping through the green. Bridwell points excitedly, and there it is, briefly visible through a sliver in the clouds, three-quarters of a mile high and swollen by storm. Various spillways pour straight off the overhanging orange cliff, merging as a uniform white shaft five hundred feet down, and turning to mist after another two thousand. The bouldered base billows like the launch pad of a moon rocket, manyfold the width of the unbridled veil. Pepe cuts speed, but the clouds block a full frontal view. As promised, Pepe says we'll again swing by, but due to the slender valley, the turn's going to be tight. Pepe grabs the mike: "Hold on, gringos, we heading back now." Pepe yanks the controls way left and the ship lists nearly on edge, Bridwell lunging for a hold as screams issue behind, drinks flying off canting trays, dozers pitching from their seats. This valley is far too narrow to safely pull a U-turn in a big, tired DC-3, and I swear we'll slam the east wall. Christ, the plane's belly seems to scrape the soggy cliff! Pepe rights the flexing, moaning plane, flashes his twelve-carat smile, then repeats the turn. More screams, more flying bodies, and that horrible creaking of over-fatigued wings.

"We're going over," shrieks Jim, not at all kidding. When we do level out, the falls are so close that spray coats the window, again obscuring our view.

"Caramba," says Pepe, "too close. We try again." And only after none-too-idle threats do we convince him otherwise. A glance behind finds the production crew in grim attitudes, limbs all over, silk shirts stained red by cheap Venezuelan wine, hands still clutching armrests, eyes wide and white. We want to razz Danny, but can't, as he is presently kissing the rug. He won't rise until a triple vodka is on his tray.

"Hey, Long," yells a cameraman, "have 'em swing by again,

eh? Couldn't see much from the carpet." Several take him seriously and scream. "No more aerobatics," sighs Bridwell.

"Amigos," laughs Pepe, relaxing the helm to light another hack, "and I thought you like adventure. You should see what happens when I'm flying alone." Pepe exhales, then crosses himself.

We land in fifteen minutes, and this, too, is hardly routine. A bump in the oiled dirt airstrip puts us temporarily airborne after the initial setdown. Despite rip-roaring rain, passengers are hopping to deplane. We notice Danny is fairly running, and, in his haste, his cobra-skin wallet has slopped from his pants and lies on the floor. Mel, Danny's boss, leans over and nabs it. A great, bovine man of resounding laugh and pleasing voice, he is a serious man, but hardly beyond a joke. Mel rakes fat fingers through his balding pate, then hands Jim the wallet. "See if you boys can't pull some kind of gag with this, eh?"

Despite the rain, the surroundings are so fantastic that Jim and I dump equipment into our thatched room, dive into swim trunks, and jam out into the eighty-degree squall. Canaima rests on the western margin of a boiling lake, this fed by the thundering La Hatcha Falls. The fifty-foot falls are a non-stop boom!, pouring forth at shocking speed to explode upon the lake they form. Great swells roll through a curtain of mist, as does a sound that locals claim is audible for 1,000 miles. It is nature in a power pose. The northbound Río Carrao flows from the dinosaur mesas east of Auyan-Tepui; running parallel, the Río Churun wanders through the Ayuan-Tepui Valley, fed by Angel and countless other falls, and joins the Carrao upon exiting the valley proper. Canaima bound, it winds through no-exit jungle and is eventually force fed through a jungled fifty-foot slot: La Hatcha Falls.

We are amazed, but it all seems passe to the Pamon Indians, the indigenous stock whose menfolk stumble about the compound. Most seem normal; some look dazed. Sighting a foot trail, we wander north through jungle so lush that passage is impossible off this path. After half an hour, we skirt the Río Carrao, now a mile above the ever-thundering La Hatcha. The rains have flooded the Carrao to within yards of the trail and would easily allow a lunatic to swim like never before, and never again.

"Say, Jim," I scream, barely audible above the falls, "how do you reckon Danny would fare in these waters?" Jim eyeballs the water charged with brutal speed and gusto. "Just fine . . . ." We plod on, quickly joined by a pathetic mongrel who nips our heels but dashes when we wheel. Enraged, Bridwell shakes a big stick, whistles suggestively while the pooch's tail wags feverishly, then chucks the stick into the Carrao. The mutt lunges, then holds up, eyeballing the racing waters, inches in front of it. Then his flea-peppered head coyly turns toward Jim with an expression that surely says, "Fuck you, Master!" The mongrel lopes on and we follow it to a crude lean-to, beneath which drone and slobber several Pamon men engaged in bizarre ritual. Initially startled, they quickly ignore us and carry on.

On a wide leaf lies a goodly mound of whitish powder – chopo, an hallucinogenic plant mixture and a staple with Pamon men.

"Holy mackerel," says Jim, believing the stash is cocaine. A stammering native scoops a sensational amount into the end of a five-foot bamboo shaft; then, with full lungs, he torpedoes the dose up the snout of the lost soul on the other end. The latter tumbles back, pawing his face, eyes spinning like roulette wheels. "Now that's a solid dose!" I exclaim. We're tempted to toot a load ourselves, but after witnessing the Pamon's pitiful stupor, we just march on. The Indians slouch back into waking dreams, sweating and retching. Later, they will stumble home to eat insubstanial food gathered through horrible labor by thankless wives. They will retch, mate, sleep – and rise to more chopo; and they will die at an early age.

That night we dine with the entire production crew. Danny is but one of many bosses and altogether subordinate to Mel, the witty and affable executive producer. After dessert, we offer Danny a Venezuelan ukelele if he'll swim La Hatcha.

"Ha!" he cracks. "Remember, you're the fools and I'm the boss; and if I say you'll be swimming them falls, you'll be swimming them falls." Danny napkins his top lip. "Anyway, how would you bums pay for that ukelele?" Laughing, Mel looks on, and his wink seems the perfect cue. I slowly draw the cobra-skin wallet from my pocket, thumbing an impressive wad of Bolivares.

"Shit, there's enough here to buy a dozen ukeleles, easy." Danny (who had called half of Canaima "thieves") flew into a tirade. "You're fired!" he screams, "you're gone on the next plane . . . ." Mel howls.

Next day we helicopter to the falls, a forty-minute, tree-level blast roughly following the Río Carrao through the flat contours of stupendous, towering jungle. Moving purely from habit, the Carrao wanders wildly and proves a poor but solitary guide. We enter the Auyan-Tepui Valley and soon land at a machete-hewn clearing two miles from Salto Angel. We quickly make for a tin-roofed shack thirty yards away, hoping to erect a telescope ere the noon clouds float in. We've got to determine the best line of descent, and, most importantly, where we will end up. In our case, once we start, there is no reversing. Danny accompanies us, much grieved, swearing that this recon is a waste of time and money. We know it is the flying that threatens him.

"Why not just chuck the ropes off and do it?" The ass. Not even a certified imbecile would try a world's record rappel over terrain he had not even seen, not when a sane rappel of only 100 feet can present all kinds of hassles.

After five minutes behind the scope, we know we are in for something nasty. Afternoon showers bloat the falls threefold, obliging our rappel to stay some distance from the cascade. This precludes us from ending up at the talus field at the fall's base – wet, but clear. Rather, we'll have to reach an overgrown terrace where we can either get plucked off by the chopper or spend weeks hacking and climbing over to the talus. On either side the falls are girdled with jungled clefts and pinnacles, so any lateral movement could take forever. In one hour, we tromp up the river to the falls, but can't make out much. We slosh back to the shack, knowing our only chance for a comprehensive view is to hover in with the chopper. But, treacherous currents, fog, and mist gust so forcefully from the base that we can't even get close. The only thing for certain is that we will have to aim for a bushy terrace one hundred feet left of the falls and hope the chopper can retrieve us. When we finally go for it, we'll know little more than when we first scanned the falls from Pepe's DC- 3.

The day arrives, and wake-up calls come at 3 A.M.; we are dumped off at the top of the falls around 7, eager to start. En route we buzz by the terrace we will shoot for, and Ron, the pilot, says he can pick us up okay so long as we hack out a twenty-by-twenty-foot clearing. Good news. We pace around on top, anxious to start what we know will be a desperate rappel. Six hours will pass as cameramen are ferried into position and loads of superfluous producers are choppered to the tin shack, for what, we can't possibly guess. A chopper floats up, deposits a cameraman, then disappears into the gathering haze.

"How much longer?" I beg.

"Be some time still," our new arrival moans, unaccustomed to such radical locales. Jim grabs the radio and summons Danny.

"Look, Ace, we gotta get going here. If we have to rappel in a downpour, it'll be pretty dicey . . . so move it!"

Danny's fractious voice barks back: "Shut your damn trap and relax; there are twelve more people yet to arrive. You'll go when I say so . . . over and out!" I glance at Jim. In genteel surroundings, Danny's guff had seemed harmless enough and we had just waved it off. Now he was looking to put us into peril, and his total disregard for anything but his commercial designs was making me hot. We paced over to the brink. A fingered water course spit through a time-worn maze of thin, mottled, limestone pillars, only to riffle off the lip and freefall three-thousand- plus feet. Daunting! Since the wall is concave, we'll soon dangle well away from the cliff, free rappelling for thousands of feet. We stand on one of a thousand golf-tee pillars, the torrent raging sixty feet below. The mist and racket here at the lip force us to jump to another pillar. This pillar's top is a soggy vegetable, littered with boulders. We wade to a roofed boulder and drier turf. A bossy voice pops over the walkie talkie. "We'll be ready for you in two minutes, Long. Stand by."

"Okay, you fools! Everyone's in position!" Several copters are hovering in patchy fog, cameras poised to record our every move. We were in a hurry, hours back; now it's drizzling and we just know an epic awaits us. But we're hardly in a position to refuse, long-jumping back to the lip. With a sad laugh, I pitch off eighteen hundred feet of rope, shoulder three six-hundred foot ropes, then back-peddle into space.

The next three hours are one continuous hassle: frightening knot transfers while twirling yards from the wall; holding positions, then racing for the cameramen; coordinating two people descending one rope, sometimes simultaneously; and always battling increasing rain. This is a mighty queer thing, this rappel. No world-class climber would do this for the fun or the accomplishment, and any "record" is pure jive. Yet the exhilaration is undeniable, and the task has put us in arguably the most novel spot I've ever been. This could almost be fun if the weather were good, but it isn't, so for the most part it's exotic misery.

The filming is over; they've got their shots, and the choppers are busily ferrying people back to Canaima. We've still got a thousand feet to go. Finally I reach a ledge above a lower-angled section, sinking knee deep into slime upon impact. Soaked through, my two Goretex parkas are like chamois. I want to stretch my numb legs, walk around a bit, but every move means sinking farther into the ooze. I muscle 600 feet of rope off my shoulder and start tossing it out. Despite careful coiling, it unravels in knots and kinks – a big twist of soppy rope. Moreover, the wall below is only eighty degrees, so no amount of coaxing can get the line to snake down uniformly – it snags on every bush and knob. Everything reminds me how crackpot this whole thing is.

"Hurry up!" yells Jim, dangling free four hundred feet above, "my harness is strangling my legs." Had we not been so waylaid, this would have proved challenge enough – in clear weather with sufficient time. Now we can barely see, the rain making routine procedures almost impossible. Still, after thirty minutes of fiddling and whining, the rope is almost untangled. Suddenly, panicked screaming! A glance upward shows Jim cuffing himself upside the head and neck, his flailing body swaying on the free-hanging line.

"It's on me! It's on me!"

Some unknown green creature with "funky barbs" has latched onto Jim's collar, and he frantically flogs it and himself into surrendering. He demands to join me on the ledge, sailing down four hundred feet at twenty-five miles per hour and plunging waist deep into the mire.

When the new rappel is set up, Jim slowly descends into the fog, the wall transforming into an off-vertical braid of lianas. When the rope comes slack, I head down.

The first three hundred feet pass smoothly, but as the lianas thicken, my ankles, wrists, and hands are continually shackled in vines. Soon the rope leads into a curving subway of creepers. I sense an unfolding scenario of meeting Jim, finding the passage closed, us sewn in shoulder tight and left to rot. A hammer, a sling, an arm snags with every downward move. It's more down clawing than rappelling. When the rope ends, leaving only the vines, I know this is the most asinine thing I've ever done.

"Say what?!" The passage ends at a ten-foot vine bridge spanning an immeasurable cleft. Just as planned, Bridwell is safe on the terrace, seventy-five feet beyond, hacking at shrubs with a machete. It is folly to ask Jim what he did here, so I slink across on hands and knees before stopping to consider. Though choked with creepers, the terrace is heaven and it shouldn't take long to clear room for a helicopter skid. But the rain is getting worse, as is the fog, and with two hours of sun left, we face the prospect of spending the night here.

I grab Jim's radio, unwrap the cellophane and start screaming. "This is Long . . . come in . . . where's the chopper? We're ready." Nothing. Finally a meek, frightened voice is just heard over the storm. It's Danny!

"The chopper is still taking people back to Canaima. It's supposed to come back, but I don't know. It's really getting wild down here. Trees are falling and it's flooding!" Danny's voice sounds like one on Death Row.

"Okay, Danny. If it does come back, make sure it gets us." Bridwell continues hacking into the foliage, trying to warm up. The storm pounds at triple forte and we have to scream to hear one another. No doubt Danny really feels the fury, for it all drains in his direction. Everything is clouded over. As bleak as a forced bivouac seems, it is maybe better than chancing a helicopter ride in such weather. But at that moment the chopper pops up through the fog, hovering a skid for us to grab. We float down to the tin hut to pick up Danny.

"Could have played soccer there," laughs Ron, the pilot, satisfied with our clearing and impervious to the weather. As we descend, the elements get angrier; but even so forewarned, we are not prepared for the havoc once we touch down at the shack.

Fuming, snorting rain rifles through an orange fog, so colored by the sun's failing glow. Previous creeks are now swollen brown cataracts, tearing and chewing through the flora. The noise and the smell – that crisp, earthy stench of destruction. Steam wafts off the ground. A sand bar washes into the river, followed by two-ton boulders, rolling, grinding downstream. I watch the torrent leap a stony bank and flush a century-old hardwood to its roots. In thirty seconds it crashes and is whisked away.

"Jesus Christ!" cracks Bridwell. The tree is one hundred feet long and careens about like a sapling. Snap! It broadsides a huge pine and only a splintered stump remains.

Terrified, Danny pitches camera gear aboard, then curls up like a pill-bug in the rear of the chopper. Ron, Jim and I shiver in swirling, ankle-deep soup, voices straining above the popping chopper blades and the squall's roaring hiss.

"Switch her off till it eases," I yell, "we'll bivvy in the chopper!" Going airborne seems mad.

"It's not gonna ease!" yells Jim, adding that he soon expects to get "T-boned" by a tree trunk. Feeling likewise, Ron wants to clear out now, pointing to the racing waters that have gnawed visible yards from our little clearing. He no doubt envisions the flood twisting his quarter-million-dollar machine into scrap metal. The water is shin deep.

"Hang here much longer and we'll be flash-flood body surfing!" screams Jim. That leaves the unthinkable. Danny remains balled up in the chopper, head buried in his legs. We pile in. Ron and Jim look confident, but something in my bones begs me to stay behind. I go along because I'm just too tired to argue. Ron clutches the stick with both hands and we whop-whop straight up, shimmying, rattling. Ron's eyes strain, neck cranes, but sees nothing – the plexiglass windshield is too fogged.

"You gotta lean out," shrieks Ron, "and tell me where the trees are!" I grab Bridwell's harness and he stretches his torso out the door. Bap! Bap! Bap! go the blades, cleaving into branches. The chopper rocks left and falters, alarm snapping across Ron's face.

"Higher, you got to go higher," Jim screams. Trees blur by, inches away.

"Can't lose sight of the fucking river," screams Ron, eyes zeroed down into the soup, "or we're goners!"

Goners? But we've just started. I figure this is a stupid comment, until I think it through. Now a series of fleet rapids, the river is our only guide back to Canaima: fifty feet wide and fading to black, it's no highway. Aside from Canaima, and the clearing we've just left, there is positively no place to set down in the jungle, which is uniformly a snug weave of treetops. There is no reversing and no stopping. We have got to gain Canaima; the river is the only way back.

Bridwell pulls his head inside, his face punished by rain and roto-wash. We switch positions. Visibility is almost nil, fog ever thickening, rain pelting down. I strain for a view, any view, but it's so damned dark and it seems a fire hose is trained on my face.

"Left! Left!," I scream, only noticing an arching banyan trunk twenty feet before impact. Ron throws the stick over. We pivot, and the tail blade thwacks off the top limbs of the hardwood.

"Watch the goddamned trees!" Ron cries, "I can't see shit. I'm flying on feel." Bridwell tries to clear the window, but everything is soaked through and he can only further smear the plexiglass. Bridwell looks back at Danny, silently curled in the fetal position.

"Give me your T-shirt," demands Jim. No reply. Again. Nothing. Finally, Jim grabs a fistful and rips it off his back, quickly turning to rub a peephole through which Ron can scout for the glint of his spotlight off the water – his only guide, save my limited lateral view.

"Sorry, Danny," adds Bridwell, honestly.

We trade places. Five minutes so positioned leaves the lookout blind and shivering. Jim leans way out, yelling fresh guesses that I scream to Ron. My legs are braced under the seat, right hand clasping Bridwell's harness, left hand rubbing Ron's ever-fogging peephole. Not a sound from Danny.

The rain has eased, but the fog has thickened; it's so dense, in fact, that the full moon brightens, but never pierces, the hanging cloud. This leaves Bridwell to decipher the tree line from the river, a lot more on hunch than fact.

"We'll never make it at this pace," Ron drolls, checking his watch, then focusing back on the water. "We've been up about fifty minutes; only got thirty minutes of fuel left." Fifty minutes? Seems more like ten. The fog has checked us to a crawl, and

Ron figures we have gone but a third of the forty miles back to Canaima. We must stay low enough to see water – our solitary guide – and centered as to avoid auguring into trees. There is no other choice but this roofless tunnel. We are moving too slowly to ever make it back, Ron assures us. And should we leave the river, we're history.

I started this jaunt hoping Ron knew something I didn't. He did not. I had no confidence at lift-off, leaving only at the urging of others. Now we're surely doomed and can only briefly defer disaster, that is if we don't crash before the fuel goes. My jaws are clenched so tightly my teeth will probably crack. "This is bullshit!" I scream into the storm, struggling to see, only because there's nothing else to do. The fog breaks for fifty feet. Silent, his mouth drawn, Ron leans over the stick and stares below.

Then a brilliant, though fog-diffused, flash, and a consequent blast of thunder. Ears pop from the pressure drop, but Ron somehow keeps her steady. Bridwell's head snaps back in, looking surprised that it should remain affixed to his shoulders. Bap! Bap!, Blades to wood. We list left, the skids drag the water, and we jerk up and right. Again the whack! of the blades, followed by another blaze and another thunderous bang. We rock left, then right, Ron screaming "watch for trees or we're going in!" Bridwell's eyes say he believes him and his head goes out again. Ron's scan never leaves the elusive sheen of his river-trained spotlight, and I wonder what it'd take to snap his concentration. Jim and I swap seats and in silent terror I lean out. Zap! A blinding yellow shaft of forked lightning jags into the river, seemingly inches before us. The concussion rolls us left, back, upside down – I don't know which way, my head rings so. The blades hack into something with such purchase that the engine stutters. Then another blast, more rocking, more hacking, and there's just no way to stay here without crashing. We've got to escape, if only to the doomed obscurity of the fog. Ron pulls the stick back and we power up, up into the clouds.

In thirty seconds we lurch out and start racing toward I don't know where. No need to scout for trees; we sit back and think. I've never been this terrified. It can only get worse. Bridwell yanks his parka over his head and emerges with a lit cigarette. He pulls hard, the red ember creeping toward his lips.

"Get the window!" yells Ron. It's ridiculous, rubbing that window. It is pitch dark and nobody sees a damn thing. There's movement behind and I turn to see Danny, his gaunt face scribed by deep and savage lines. His lips move but say nothing. He's a wretched individual, so I pity him all the more. For the previous week I'd been so enchanted with the jungle's raw energy that I hadn't stopped to consider what a terrible and oppressive effect it could have on others – others whose conception of wilderness is a potted fern in the corner of their condo. Danny had stepped from a Hollywood sound stage straight into the jungle. The whisper of a gnat's wings could set him running. The thunder had slain his final guard. Eyes burning, his twisted features make the perfect death mask. A chill tracks my spine and the rain keeps pounding.

The fog sporadically breaks; we are buzzing through little windows of moonlit space, then burrowing back into clouds. Light and darkness flicker by, acknowledging that we are moving at top speed. Ron powers on, jaw fixed, leaving us to guess his plan, should he have one. Bridwell lights another smoke, Danny curls back up – now just a trembling corpse. A rising terror is starting to unman me, too. Ron presumably tires of the fog and gently pulls the stick back. We soon pop up and out into shiny space. Below, spread out over the night, the cloud bank extends perpetually, an eerie silvered mirror, upon which the bursting overhead moon hurls our fleeting shadow. Periodic lightning clicks on like stage lights. What are we doing, other than going nowhere fast? Ron remains silent. Finding this unbearable, I force a confidence. He thumbs the moisture off the compass and starts in reedy gasps.

"All I can do is take a heading . . . which is towards Canaima. We'll never find it without the river...we gotta find the river." For the first time I read the uncertainty on Ron's face. Bridwell exhales a stream of Camel smoke: "You got x-ray eyes or something?"

"Fuck you!" spits Ron. Now I know he's desperate. But Jim's right; we'll find nothing up here. Realizing this, and our right to know the plan, Ron continues, pausing between lines. We will carry on at speed, making up lost time, doing so until the fuel light blinks on. That means ten minutes – ten minutes to find a shaft through the clouds, then to find the river, then to find Canaima. Ron taps at the fuel gauge, needle twitching just off the E.

"Five minutes, then it's reserve."

My mind races, calculates, guesses, spins. Five minutes, fifteen total. How far have we come? How long at speed? How many miles left? With every passing second, Ron's plan seems more of a long shot. The doubts are chewing on my brain. After several minutes, we ease back into the fog and continue, dead blind, Ron's eyes bouncing between instruments. Danny has not moved or made a sound. The engine wails, but the absence of screaming, bantering, and cursing effects a deafening silence.

Bridwell stares at me, puts his hand to his forehead, then forces a laugh. "Can you believe this?" I also force a laugh, which is more of an animated sob. The strain of a long and involved day has torn me down. Without the fulcrum of future hopes, doors fly open to my most private vaults: my folks, things I never did that I swore I would, kids I'll never have, questions I have never answered. I'm feeling so sorry for myself. Melancholy. Hey! I ain't shoveling coal yet! If I'm to die, I'll go out cussing, scratching, biting, kicking . . . .

The fuel light flashes on and my terror is reinstated tenfold. I start rubbing the window, clutching Jim's harness as he leans way, way out, searching for that bright shaft. Again we are lost in the fray. I'm totally, absolutely, indescribably horrified – but, oddly, I like it, feeling three hundred percent alive. The fog is sparse but multilayered, and that we should find a window through is something I'm begging God to grant. Godsent or not, one appears out left.

"Hold on!" screams Ron, manhandling the stick. We roll, then dive, soon skimming the treetops, clear and moonlit. Clouds soon hover fifty feet above. The rain pelts through but the moonlight does not, so navigation is so much guesswork. Bap! Bap! Top branches.

"Watch the trees!" I lean out, winching, half expecting the bruising impact of a high bough. Half my body is levered out, Bridwell with a waist lock. Ron's spotlight pans about and when it bounces off green, I yell accordingly. Visibility is pathetic, and considering our daring nearness to the trees we keep kissing, the odds are stacked that some supreme tree will take us out. A rise in terrain and we're finished. We hold course and are soon released into moonlit space. Jim takes the watch. My hand reaches for his harness and shakes like the palsy. Light still dancing, Ron slows, his eyes fixed below. A glint. We descend, lower, lower. Water. The river!

Ron throws the stick over and we are down, skimming the rapids in reasonable moonlight. Whether through fluke, deity, or Ron's jungle savvy, we've quickly hurtled two of three obstacles and are in the best position to find Canaima. But it's not to be. The fog returns. Bridwell again leans out; I start rubbing the windshield again; and we again start to crawl, blades thwacking into wood. When the panel starts momentarily buzzing, it's like a bullwhip.

"We'll never make it doing this!" screams Ron. "Pull him in!" Bridwell looks disappointed, as he's never learned to quit. Ron powers up one hundred feet and lets her fly. Every two seconds the panel throws its tantrum.

"Five minutes," yells Ron. Should there appear any sign of Canaima, we'll never see it. We race on into darkness. Then the fog clears and we jump at how close we are to the trees. The river gleams below, but rather than chug it at water line, we track a straight line, ripping past the river's elbows, begging Canaima to show its face, while knowing we're wishing upon a star. The dark expanse reaches far into the cool and rainy night. I cringe with each buzz from the panel. The galaxy is jammed into my skull, and expands with every move, second, sound, buzz. When Ron says we're probably following the wrong river, I start psyching for the crash.

zzzz! zzzz! zzzz! whines the panel. Bridwell's hands clench and relax, clench and relax. If a branch or lightning swats us down, I reckon this is survivable, from the river anyway. Enduring a crash through the sky-scraping trees will require springy limbs and some luck, yet this too seems possible, even probable. But once marooned, we'd be history: no food, no bearings, no prayer. The trees will sigh, leaves will fall, and no vestige will remain.

"How can this be the wrong river?" I plead, slamming my fist on the seat. The map shows only the Río Carrao, but who know what springs up in a typhoon?

Ron's head snaps left, gaping into the night. You'd think he'd spotted El Dorado. He cocks an ear, cracks a faint smile, then punches the throttle down. The chopper screams at maximum speed, tach needle pegged in the red. Even above the engine I hear it. Initially faint, but soon an inimitable roar. There may flow other rivers, but there's only one La Hatcha Falls – one quarter mile from Canaima. We lurch over a rise and explode at the glow of Canaima's few lights, one-half mile farther. Simultaneously, the panel's buzz becomes continuous.

"One minute!" cries Ron, hunched over the stick, squinting, face wrenched by the drama. I elbow Jim in the ribs. It's down to the wire.

We've got one minute until we crash but it shouldn't take more than forty-five seconds to find the landing spot, though we now re-enter the fog as I hang out shouting directions like I actually know where to go, and that emergency buzzer is torture, for we can only guess whether we're above the clearing, because it's raining like hell and Ron's spotlight bounces off the fog, leaving him to guess whether it's ten or fifty feet to the ground, and the engine starts hacking as Danny finally rises and screams wildly and if this hasn't been the longest two hours I can't imagine what would be.

A Stone from Allah

I WANTED TO GET TO THE END of the world, or at least so close I could see it. Rick would do the organizing and raise the money. He'd twice been to Everest and knew something about putting such a trip together. Well into my twenties, I had never been off the American continent, which disturbed me. As a kid I'd slept with maps and National Geographics, had worshiped a globe-trotter who came to my high school with films of kayaking the Blue Nile and trekking across Afghanistan. After a couple of us went hiking with him in the Sierras, we aped his every move, down to the way he spit, and I vowed to become a world explorer. Then I started rock climbing and for ten years rarely left California. Now I wanted to change all that with one expedition.

Rick suggested Borneo for two reasons: He had a powerful friend in Jakarta who'd made three probes to Borneo's interior, long considered the wildest place left on earth. Clayton Porter knew all the logistics, and could arrange the requisite papers to enter one of Indonesia's off limits islands. Second, Borneo had the right ring, would conjure the carnival image of the fearsome headhunter – rabid, tattooed, surviving on live rats his master chucked into his cage. This, Rick knew, would capture corporate ears and hopefully, corporate dollars. So I started frequenting

the U.C.L.A. library, combing through moth-eaten anthropol-
ogical tomes, gleaning enough hard information to write a
captivating proposal.

My proposal was a pack of lies. I quoted liberally from the old
tomes but found that even the ripest passages lacked the desired
flair; so I shamelessly embellished them, even made up entire
rituals, particularly about headhunting which, as I quoted ficti-
tious experts, was in steady practice as I wrote. Looking back
it's astounding anyone could believe in two pound fire ants or
midget cannibals. But they bought it all and Rick got the money.
The curious, perhaps fitting effect was, as our departure grew
closer, I started believing my own hogwash, dreaming of flashing
machetes and prehistoric rodents and a river that pitched underground – the same, unexplored river we had pledged to raft
down for five hundred miles.

When I met the rest of the expedition in San Francisco I had a
case of nerves that all the free drinks on our Singapore flight
couldn't settle. Twenty hours later, when we touched down in
Jakarta and the first wave of tropical swelter washed over me, I
was so edgy that should someone have touched me from behind,
they'd have had to peel me off the airport ceiling with a blow-
torch. Bouncing through Jakarta in a sputtering cab made things
worse. All the brown bodies, millions of them, scampering
through the madness like ants looking for a hole. Great mosques
reared off this vast and smouldering squalor; from speakers on
their gleaming domes droned the bizarre incantations of Moslem
muzzens. The heat was ferocious and my shirt was soaked
through. It all seemed surreal, threatening, and paranoia gripped
me because I was soon bound for darkest Borneo where I stood
a fifty-fifty chance of getting my head filched. A really asinine
notion, but I believed it just then, and probably deserved to.

When we arrived at Clayton's home, a mansion in central
Jakarta, I mellowed slightly, but not much. Clayton was incredible. Inside the compound where he and a dozen other expatriots
lived, he led the life of a Rajah. He had a dozen servants, one
whose sole duty was looking after his parrots! Clayton was a live
wire with fantastic buoyancy minus the pomp of the Harvard
lawyer he was. Quick with a drink and even quicker with a joke,
there's not a man alive who would peg him as the legal brains

behind Indonesian policy. But he was, and rallied by our arrival he insisted we straightaway bolt for the Otman bar, where "the beer is light and the women are dark." That was music to my partners' ears, but I was so rattled that I passed, citing jet lag and a headache. Alone in that big house I grew even more spooked, for Clayton was keen on native artifacts, and every inch of wall bore ghastly masks, carved spear-toting savages, and huge beasts with hideous human heads and jagged shark's teeth. And there was no escaping their leer – not in the bathroom, the closet – they were everywhere; and dammit to hell I was going into the heart of darkness and I was going to die! I paced like a crazy man. But without sleep in fifty hours, nature shut me down. I poured down two bottles of Bintang, stretched out and was gone.

When I woke I didn't know who or where I was. I knew even less of the gorgeous brown Java girl who straddled me, slapped me, and laughed out a gusher of Bahasa of which I understood not word one. The boys were well lit, had hustled a bevy of beautiful girls back to the house for a night of debauchery. Clayton shoved a bottle into my hand and howled:

"I defy you to sleep tonight, old man. Have fun while you still can. Best to have some good memories to take where you're going . . . ."

On his last trip to Borneo Clayton caught dengue fever and it damn near killed him. I pressed the girl off me, jumped up, and shuttered. My partners had several Java girls fawning over each of them. They babbled a steady torrent of Bahasa at Clayton, who translated for both parties, taking great pleasure in putting his own angle on the reply. Slowly, various odd pairings meandered off to different rooms. One big buxom girl had my buddy Jim to herself, though a younger, angelic girl who had hung to the shadows now fastened herself to the bigger girl's side – looking scared and confused. When Jim and the buxom one went to leave, the younger girl tagged along behind. The older girl shouted at her, then pushed the girl at me. Then she and Jim left.

The younger girl kept her distance, staring at me. I saw the terror in her eyes. Perhaps she saw the same in mine. I motioned her to sit down, then dug out my Indonesian/English dictionary, hoping she could divert my fears. I didn't want to unnerve this girl, who I put at about sixteen. Starving, I looked up the word for food. In minutes we had rifled Clayton's freezer and were cooking up a big pot of rice and fish. She relaxed a bit. As she ate, she never took her eyes off me. And she ate like she hadn't in a month. Afterwards we moved to a couch where, under the poised hatchet of a wooden Asmat warrior, I tried talking to her, one looked-up word at a time. No, I wasn't married. A search through my wallet found no smiling couples so I guess she believed me. First hesitating, she showed me her wallet, which had a few 100 Rupiah notes worth 20 cents and an identification card on which I was surprised to see "Djena Ketut" listed as nineteen. Djena liked the feel of that card, which bore her picture under a plastic heat seal. She put her finger on the card then on her chest to make certain I knew that photo was her. Her simplicity was so disarming that sometime in there I quit fretting about Borneo. We were both enjoying ourselves, had calmed the other down. Feeling relaxed, then drowsy, I moved toward my assigned room: Djena followed, probably afraid the big, buxom girl would cuff her if she didn't. When I stripped down to trunks, she started trembling; but when I put my hands up indicating I had no designs on her, she relaxed altogether, wouldn't let me sleep, and made me try and talk some more. I could see she was uneasy about the sounds coming through the walls.

For a moment I just looked at her. Her hair and eyes were jet black. Blinding white teeth and soft lips graced a cherubic face, the kind of face which, the more you explore it, the more perfect it becomes. Her skin was like God. When a Java girl grows lovely, she is worth thrashing fifty miles through a bramble patch to look upon. Hard times had ground a marked humility into her, but that only increased her charm. And all she wanted to do was talk, because she was frightened. Understanding her fleet lingo was like trying to sight-read the Rosetta Stone, but we got by with patois and body language. I don't know what set the bond that night – less how to define it. Maybe just the cant of an eye, or folded hands, or the timbre of a laugh; more likely just a certain ease born of natural affinities, the why of which we weren't meant to know anyway. Whatever, after another hour I had completely forgotten about Borneo.

Then she pulled something from her pocket and, cupping it in her hands, briefly pondered it. Curious, I leaned over. She extended her hands and in the hollow I saw a wee stone. I took it and held it up to the light. It was just a little polished agate, like you find on fobs, or key chains. I saw she was very happy about this shiny little stone, so I smiled. Then for the first time she smiled, as wide of the milky way. I kissed her forehead, then laid my head down. She got behind me, wrapped her arms around my chest and hung on for the night.

The next morning we were awakened by the big buxom girl who yelled at Djena to get a move on, then left. I'd overslept and the boys were anxious to plough into town and buy the last supplies we'd need for Borneo. Oh yes, Borneo . . . . When I got out of the shower Djena was still waiting for me, though the buxom girl was screaming at her to leave. She just wanted to say goodby again; then smiling, she held out the little stone for a last look but the fellows were hollering so just then I couldn't be bothered with the stone. I told her to come back that night and we'd eat a kilo of food together. She looked lost, sadly tucked the stone back into her pocket and left.

In an offhand way I mentioned the stone business to Clayton as we ate dinner, waiting for the girls to arrive. Clayton laughed, said these stones were highly prized among the very poor who, like everyone else, loved owning something handsome and valuable, but could only afford a little polished agate. Such stones weren't worthless, he promised, for the good ones (he laughed again here) cost upwards of five dollars. Sort of a poor man's diamond. Something hurt inside me when I realized Djena was trying to share with me the beauty of her only possession, something I probably wouldn't have even picked up had I seen it in the gutter. Reflecting on that lost look of hers was like being whipped.

Clayton took up a collection for the girls. They were his friends, and he treated friends well. Sure, they had other friends, but Clayton was their favorite. He assumed, incorrectly, that since we'd all had our way with them we should give them some money. Fair is fair; plus, it was their only means of support. Clayton also mentioned that the big buxom girl was Djena's cousin. Djena had been forced from her home in Bandung because her parents were so poor they could barely feed them-selves. So Djena had come to live with her cousin. This was normal, not tragic, and by Javanese standards Djena had been fortunate to enjoy her parents' thatched roof for ninteen years. Many are turned out at thirteen, or married off to a Bukas traitor with a handful of Rupiah or a few rugs from Sumba. Djena had only been in Jakarta a week and was slow in adopting her cousin's livelihood. Nor was she bringing down any money, which left the cousin to support them both. Things would change. The boys were certain things had, knew I was good for some Rupiah. They ribbed me about "breaking her in". I didn't say anything. I just wanted to see Djena and admire her stone, then her, and try and forget about the career waiting for her and the crouching cannibal waiting for me.

The girls turned up, all but Djena. The cousin said she was sick of Djena's sulking and had left her at home. Her place was within walking distance so I made the cousin draw a crude map, then I set out on foot. "Don't expect the Taj Mahal", Clayton laughed. For two hours I battled through a maze of alleys and criss-crossing walkways, teeming with little brown kids and big black insects, elbowing past countless little shops where toothless Chinamen hawked sarongs and cheap batiks, through clouds of burning cloves, past eateries on wheels where the woks burned hot and the smell of sate mixed with the fetor of excrement and dead dogs floating in the stream behind me. I showed the map to a dozen people who regarded me as a Martian, but I found the place eventually.

What a place! Tin walls and a dirt floor. A cot for the cousin, while Djena slept atop a blanket straight on the dirt. But Djena made that little hovel shine. She was so surprised and excited that she scurried around in a circle trying to divert my eyes from the abject surroundings but I just half motioned, half told her to simmer down and let me have a look at that mighty fine stone. She smiled like the milky way again and handed me the agate. I held it like the Hope Diamond and Djena looked the happiest person in Asia and I wasn't far behind her.

During the next two days I spent all free moments and both nights with Djena. Fifty dollars got the cousin off her back and I managed to postpone her inevitable profession, though sometimes I was talking through gritted teeth. Still, we had an intimacy which had eluded me with women I'd lived with for two years running. Time and need had conspired to serve up the perfect gift. There was nothing dramatic about our fellowship, spent in harmless little trifles like trying to catch a gecko inside my room, or thumbing through a picture book Clayton had on Germany. We were tonic for each other; both scared, both uncertain, but happy in spite of it. So I launched off to Borneo, not with a belly full of terror but with memories fond enough to carry me through – and bring me back.

The first coast-to-coast traverse of Borneo was the stuff of dreams. The fierce Dyak cannibals were amongst the best natured people I'd ever met, hadn't fleeced a head in forty years. The jungle had a mythical sweep and beauty that took us back to a time when the world was fantastically young and raw. In the dark bosom of the primordial interior, I'd never felt so alive. Of course a two month epic had it's trials. A week after missionaries had flown Rick out with typhoid, we charged into the central divide, a nightmare of monsoon, leeches, and hateful rip-saw vines, where orangutans screeched in the towering brawl of treetops while we trudged on and on through the dim and steaming mulch below. Yet it was wonderful.

By sheer fluke, while snug in the very center of unexplored rain forest, the topic of the little polished stone came up. Edwin, an English-speaking Javanese who was traversing along with us, explained that while the stones were indeed cherished as a valuable possession, there was much more to it. South of Jakarta, in Bandung, there is a fountain said to flow with Allah's blood. Not his actual blood, but with something similar to the wine in a Eucharist celebration. When the stones are passed through the sacred waters, they become a talisman of good fortune for the keeper. Should the stone get lost, all one's luck is lost as well. It's unheard of to give such stones away, for when the stone changes hands, both fortune and hope are transferred with the gift. So Djena's little polished agate took on even greater purpose.

We were lost half the time, but we reached Tatakan on the East coast in sixty days. The traverse was history. We made it back to Clayton's two days later and I went straight to Djena's place. I was twenty pounds lighter, was punctured, bitten, torched, bone-weary with a second degree burn on my hand. Djena burst into tears and fairly threw me onto the cot to start rubbing all manner of fragrant salves onto my abrasions – which were many, none serious. She looked as beautiful as before, but seeing the hard corners of her mouth I knew she had finally found her way around the Otman bar. She also had bruises about her neck and arms, but I didn't ask why. Sad though it was, it relaxed me, for it somehow put us on equal footing.

So there we were to nurse each other's wounds: mine from faking the explorer, hers from getting passed around the Otman bar to sate men three times her age and twice her weight for the few Rupiah they'd pry from their pockets. She slept with a death grip on my chest, kissed every inch, or nearly every inch of my body. Yet during all our nights together, I never laid a hand on her. Not in a sexual way, you understand. And it's not rectitude that kept me at bay. From Jakarta we went to Tokyo where I spent my last dollar in the Geisha house. It's just that we both needed another kind of healing. Our magic came from the fact that we didn't know each other at all but honored one another like the last person on earth. I don't doubt she would have been the finest night of my life. Her sighs could kill a man.

After two months in Borneo my Bahasa was up to pidgin level, painful in one regard because Djena was telling me things that were hard to deal with. Whatever self-respect she had now lay on the floor of the Otman bar. Yet she wasn't just a poor little native girl forced into perdition through need. She was this, yes, but though she'd spend her prime on her back, she'd do so with clinched fists and a heart barred to them all. While she tried to block all that out she broke down the last night and it took an hour of cajoling to draw her out of it. But she would never come out of it, and she would never see me again. Knowing this, and because her heart knew no boundaries, she tried to give me the little polished agate, to remember her by.

I studied the stone, tumbling it in my fingers, knowing I couldn't take the most precious thing she had. Strangers had taken her soul and she wanted to give me all she had left: all her fortune and the little luck the stone could preserve of her otherwise cursed existence. She said her dreams were silly girl dreams, that her hopes were few and her luck was scant; but they were marvelous and magical inside her head and she didn't want them wasted. With her they'd only evaporate, like Djarun smoke in the dark alleys. But if I'd take her dreams they'd live on with the luck of the stone, and I'd have fortune and happiness. My heart dropped through my shoes. I realized in one respect she was blessed, more fortunate than the rest of us. I'd never know a passion so strong that I would sacrifice everything in its name. I had often pondered, and had finally met the person who would throw their body on the grenade to save the other guy. The rest of us claw from the fox hole, will do anything to avert Djena's kind of passion. The rest of us keep the stone.

So I told Djena one of the few things in my life that I'm really glad I said: That she was going to keep that stone, forever. That our lives would be full of wonderful things, like our friendship. But there would be wretched moments when people would hurt us, when we'd starve for more than food. And when life seemed hopeless, I told her to gaze at that little polished stone – to remember what it held for us both, that we had treated each other kindly, made one another feel comfortable in the face of fears, uncertainty, and discomfort. And she smiled like the Milky Way.

You'll never know how many times I've called on that stone.